THE COUNTRY MAID

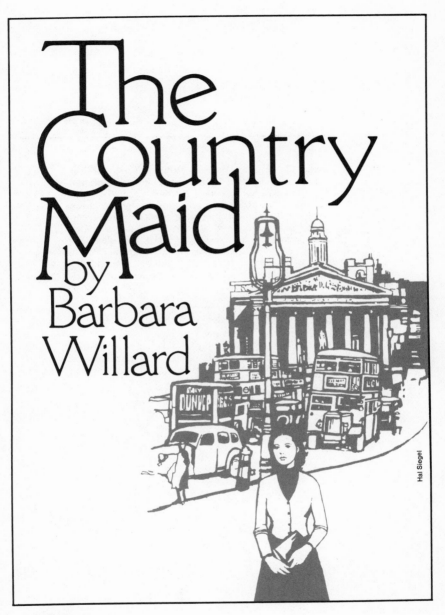

The Country Maid

by Barbara Willard

Hal Siegel

 GREENWILLOW BOOKS, New York

First American Edition   1 2 3 4 5 6 7 8 9 10

Library of Congress Cataloging in Publication Data
Willard, Barbara.   The country maid.
Summary: A 16-year-old, who has left her home in the
English countryside to go into service with a London fam-
ily in the 1930's, gradually realizes what she really wants.
[1. Servants—Fiction   2. England—Fiction]
I. Title. PZ7.W6547Cr 1980   [Fic]   79-19002
ISBN 0-688-80256-7

THE COUNTRY MAID

1

"THERE ARE just the four of us," Mrs. Garside said. "You need not worry, Mrs. Martle, about her being overworked."

"No, I am sure not, madam," the other woman replied. "Of course it'd be her first place. But I know she was always a good girl helping at home. There's two of her sisters in service and very nicely placed. And she's quite a fair cook. Aren't you, Cassie?"

Sitting on the edge of her chair, her hands clasped rigidly together on her knees, Cassie gave a flickering smile. It seemed not quite the thing to nod, thus implying Yes, I am a good cook. She glanced quickly at Mrs. Garside and then away. Mrs. Garside looked a nice, friendly lady; she was not too old, but not too young, either, and whatever her age might be was rather pretty. It was summer and she wore a short light dress with a flowery pattern. Her thick hair was a reddish brown, worn short, not exactly shingled, more a sort of bob. Cassie liked it that way, though she could see that it was a bit old-fashioned. Mrs. Garside seemed to match the room, Cassie thought, a room that was comfortable but not rich, the curtains and covers light and greenish, the carpet rather worn. There were some books that would be a nuisance to dust, but not too many bits and pieces—not like The Laurels back home, where Marge had worked; in the drawing room there you couldn't see the shelves for the ornaments.

"What did you call her, Mrs. Martle?" Mrs. Garside was asking Cassie's stepmother. "Cassie?" She gave a kind of frowning smile. "Is it short for something else? Or a nickname?"

"Her name's Cassandra, madam."

"Oh dear—I don't think we can call her that! Has she a second name?"

"Cassandra's always been a lot in the family, it seems," Mrs. Martle said. She did not speak slightingly, she did not join Mrs. Garside's smiling. Rather, she spoke with a curious kind of dignity. Cassie thought it good of her to stand up for a name she might easily have thought outlandish. After all, she was only very shortly a member of the family and might easily have sided with Cassie's possible employer.

"Tell Madam your other name, dear," she said, in a supporting sort of voice.

"Edith," said Cassie, reluctantly.

"Then I think you had better be Edith—that is, if we decide that you are to come to us."

At this Cassie's whole world vanished in mist before her. She screwed her fingers together and her gloves, that were a bit silky, faintly squeaked. She knew herself to be a strange girl called Edith existing in a strange place among strangers. She saw her stepmother liking Mrs. Garside and kindhearted enough to feel relieved and glad

2

of that—yet nonetheless casting off Cassie so that only Edith, nicely settled, would be left behind. . . .

"Well," said Mrs. Garside, rising from the sofa, where she had been rather gracefully seated with one arm stretched along the back, "I shall just have a word with my husband. But I know he will agree with me. Shall we say next Monday, Mrs. Martle? She will have every Wednesday afternoon and evening, and every other Sunday. I suggest twelve and sixpence a week and I shall supply her uniform."

"Thank you, madam, that seems very satisfactory," said Mrs. Martle.

The two women smiled at one another. Mrs. Martle looked respectful—but so, indeed, did Mrs. Garside. "A very nice, sensible woman," she would surely say to her husband. . . . She went with them to the door. This time next week Cassie—Edith—would be opening it. Then they were outside in Stanton Avenue, walking up past houses that were all alike, and coming to the main road where the buses conveniently stopped on the corner. Mrs. Martle held Cassie by the arm but seemed unable to find anything to say until they were standing at the bus stop.

"A very nice, sensible lady," she said, changing only one word of Cassie's imagining, but such a word as tore the world in two.

Slowly but with brutal steadiness the tears began to trickle down Cassie's cheeks.

"Oh there!" cried her stepmother, making a clumsy, rejected move to enfold her. "I know, dear, I know how

3

you feel. But we've all got to grow up, one way or another —and you're fully sixteen."

The Garsides were indeed four in family, just as the advertisement in the paper-shop window had said and as Mrs. Garside had confirmed. Besides Mr. and Mrs. Garside there was Miss Jean and Master Rodney. Miss Jean was a tall, plain but sometimes funny girl of eighteen; Master Rodney could have been a changeling —he was a mere six years old, which meant that his sister at this moment in their joint lives was three times his age. Cassie's own family was a large one. It struck her as barely believable that a girl of eighteen should have a brother of six, without there being at the very least a couple or so dead ones in between; but it soon appeared that this was not so. When Cassie arrived on the Monday, with her goods in a straw basket neatly strapped and labeled C. E. MARTLE, Miss Jean was standing in her bedroom doorway as Mrs. Garside led the newcomer upstairs. Her door and the door of Cassie's room were side by side. As soon as she saw her mother appear at the head of the stairs, Miss Jean turned smartly into her own room and closed the door.

"Here we are, Edith. I've made new curtains for you, look. It's rather a little room, but I think there's enough space for a girl of your size." She smiled as she spoke. She looked the least bit anxious. She wants me to be happy, Cassie thought; and in a rebellious way half regretted having nothing, so far, to hate. "Do you like them, Edith? The curtains?"

"They're very pretty. Thank you, madam," Cassie said.

They were, in fact, very pretty indeed, having small groups of trees set upon individual knolls, with a bird or two flying between.

"I hope you'll settle down with us, Edith. I know you are a long way from home—but we all want you to be happy here. There's a nice, light kitchen for you. I'm sure you'll be quite comfortable there when you are off duty. Have you brought some paper and envelopes? I expect you'll be wanting to write home. Anyway, if you've none of your own I can let you have some."

Cassie did not answer this. She saw the small garden from the window—the green, the just-finished daffodils, the apple tree. The house stood in the very last row built this side of London. Beyond the enclosing fences lay acre upon acre of fruit trees, now in bloom. You could have walked all the way into the distance on their frothing tops, so Cassie thought. Home came into her mind and she looked quickly away from the memory and from the view. Then among those trees, undaunted by creeping London, the cuckoo called. Cassie broke into smiles and turned impulsively.

"He sound near as he do at ours," she said.

"Well, there," Mrs. Garside said. "There's a welcome for you!"

And as if her cares had lightened at this exchange, she knocked on the next door—a notice pinned to it warned PRIVATE—and called to her daughter.

"Jean! Just a minute, dear."

The door opened, and the tall girl stood, leaning against the jamb, as shy as Cassie, but able to disguise it with a slightly swaggering air. Her mother said that this was

Edith, who had come from the country to look after them. Miss Jean smiled at Cassie and Cassie said, "Good afternoon, miss."

"Good afternoon," said Miss Jean.

Then she was silent.

"Well," said Mrs. Garside, "I expect you'd like to unpack your things, Edith. When you come down I'll show you where everything is and then perhaps you could get us some tea."

"Yes," said Cassie. "Yes, madam."

The advent of a third party had stirred her up a bit. She went quite briskly into her room, closing the door behind her and for the first time finding a place altogether her own; at home she shared the little room under the roof with Queenie. Humming unexpectedly, she began to stow her belongings in the drawers and the cupboard. They took up rather little room, but with twelve and sixpence a week to spend, she would soon have lots more clothes and things to fill up the space.

After five minutes or so she heard the next door open and then there was a tap on her own. There stood Miss Jean, holding something in her hand which she thrust toward Cassie.

"I thought you might like this alarm clock, Edith."

"Thank you." Cassie heard the hint of suspicion in her voice.

"You're sure to be up before I am. So you could just bang on my door when you go down to get the breakfast." As Cassie did not reply, she said, "Is that all right, Edith?"

"Yes, miss. It's just I'm Cassie first and Edith second. So I don't hear Edith when you say it."

"Cassie's much nicer! Much! I'm sure I shall call you Cassie."

Cassie did not answer. Miss Jean struck her as a rather funny sort. She might be nice or she might be nasty. Cassie reserved judgment on this matter. She took the clock. She had a wristwatch, but that would not wake her in the mornings. The two stood awkwardly, neither knowing the right moment to turn away. Then Miss Jean said, "Well . . ." and went rather fast down the stairs, singing in a suitable, crooning fashion, "A turn to the right, and a little white light, Will lead you to My—blue —heaven. . . ."

Although No. 15 Stanton Avenue was a very small house—semidetached, as the estate agents called it—the kitchen was quite big. It was almost twice the size of Gran's, where six of them had lived most of their life from the day their mother died. That kitchen was crowded even when no one was in it, for there had to be seats for them all, and a table big enough where everyone could eat. As you stepped down into it out of the sunshine you stepped into a cave of warmth and familiarity, the windows filled up with tall geraniums so that light had to come from the open door, or from the fire glowing in the kitchen range. On the rag mat before the range the old dog, Danny, would certainly be curled, and in the basket chair close by, the tortoiseshell Puss. It was ordinary, you could visit a score of cottages in the street and they would be much the same. Some had more children and some had more dogs and cats, and most were visited by the family hens, looking in through the back scullery door to see that all was as usual, then moving off, muttering gently as they went. . . . Here in Mrs. Garside's kitchen, everything was different. Of course there were no hens, but there was no dog, either. There was Miss Jean's cat, a lean black-and-white very ready to dispense affection where it seemed most advantageous.

"He knows which side his paws are buttered," Miss Jean had said, that very first evening.

Cassie smiled, chasing the joke through her imagination but finding little sense in it.

"He do seem friendly. What name's he got?"

"Pushkin."

"Come on, then, Pusskin," said Cassie.

"Pushkin," Miss Jean had corrected.

"I see," said Cassie. She had not and never would, that was certain. "Come on, then, good Pusskin," she had whispered, when Miss Jean had gone away.

The kitchen, in fact, pleased Cassie by its difference from any she had known. The walls were white, the curtains were made from red check gingham, there was a basket chair with two cushions, one red, one blue. Everything was tidy. The cupboard held rows of jars, all clean; the cooker shone; there was a comfortable coke stove in the corner; the larder was cool; the small clock ticked busily; there was a calendar with a picture of a huge man in old-fashioned clothes and three women grouped round him, all laughing. The calendar was one of those with a leaf to tear off for every day of the year. On each leaf there was the date and the day and a quotation. Before she went to bed that first evening of her coming, Cassie pulled off the day's date, reading the

8

quotation. "Times change," it said, "and we with time, But not in ways of friendship."

Out of the jumble of her worries, Cassie thought briefly of Ned. . . .

On the evening of her second day, Cassie sat at the scrubbed kitchen table—covered with a cloth that matched the curtains, to make it look more comfortable, Mrs. Garside had said—and wrote her first letter home. She addressed the envelope first, while she was still fresh and her handwriting at its best. As she wrote very carefully the familiar names, the place leaped before her—the wide village street, the old houses, the carts rumbling, the water meadows, the river, the big church. Her mouth opened slightly, as if in a soundless cry. Then she shut it firmly, and restoring her pride, wrote at the head of the sheet that Mrs. Garside had given her—she had given the envelope, too, ready stamped—her own present address: 15, Stanton Avenue, London, S.W.

"Dear Gran," she wrote. . . . If she closed her eyes, Gran would turn, ladle in hand, from the kitchen range, turning quickly as she always did, turning swiftly to welcome, turning, her sharp brown face just smiling, her bright dark brown eyes that sometimes you could catch when they were soft with caring, but at the moment of any greeting merry and sly. "That's you, Cassie . . . ?" Or Margery, or Leslie, or whoever she expected. . . .

"Dear Gran, I am well as I hope you are. And the others. I come here with Mum last Monday so now I am earning. Mrs. Garside seem nice. Miss Jean all right the little boy is a tinker he is six year old and have dark curly hair. Miss Jean is eighteen year old and none between.

9

Miss Jean is not pretty she have fair hair but not gold like our Queenie. I am here in this nice pretty kitchen it is hardly like a kitchen and I think of you. And the others. Gran, please write or tell Queenie write and tell all that goes at ours. Your loving child, Cassie."

Of course she was not really Gran's *child*, but Gran always called the six of them her children, as if there had been no one before them to claim her attention—only Margery and Jack, Leslie and Amy, Queenie and Cassandra.

"PS," wrote Cassie, forming her letters once again with great care, "tell Ned Gooderham. . . ." She paused. Tell him what? "Tell Ned Gooderham here is a piece of London though you might not know it from the fruit trees. I like it here, say."

She wanted him to know. Walking down by the river, along the water swollen by springtime, she had told him she was going away. "My dad's new wife invite me. London. I can get work there, so she tell."

She saw still his astonished face and the gaping way, like a young bird, he had seemed struggling to answer but could find no words. So she wrote: "I like it here, say."

She slid the letter into the envelope, licked the flap and sealed it very carefully. Then she remembered that she had told Gran nothing about Mr. Garside. She hesitated, wondering about a second PS. But she would surely spoil the envelope and that would mean asking for another. Anyway—what in the world was Gran to make of Mr. Garside?

Cassie rose from the table, the cane chair creaking like a swing in a mulberry tree. Then she paused, astonished, even shocked, by the sudden recognition of having lost her freedom. She had almost opened the door and walked straight out. But she was Edith, in service to Mrs. Garside, and must ask permission.

The sitting-room door stood just open. Mrs. Garside was sewing, Miss Jean as usual reading. She sat sideways in her chair, her feet twisted round her ankles, the book held close as if she loved it so well she not only read the words in it but smelled and heard and tasted them. She held it, Cassie might have thought, had she gone so far in her opinions and expressions, as if she needed it. The wireless was playing. Music.

Cassie tapped on the door, saying with faultless politeness, "Excuse me, madam, I am now going to the post."

Mrs. Garside looked up from her sewing. She seemed a little surprised by such a firm statement. "The post? Ah— you've written your letter. Very well. The post goes in fifteen minutes. Run along then. But come straight back, Edith."

Forgetting any further refinements, Cassie turned and almost ran from the house. She heard Mrs. Garside call after her, "Come straight back." Miss Jean made some remark, her voice raised. Didn't like being disturbed in her reading, perhaps—or had she said, "Don't *fuss*, mother!"

It was an evening in advance of its date—the end of April, the air soft and warm, the sky cloudless and swinging with ten-o'clock stars, yet below it nothing better than the dull little streets, the traffic heard faintly and spasmodically from the main road. On the corner of Stanton Avenue and Blenheim Gardens a street lamp stood sentinel to the red pillar box. Its curly initials that stood for King George V were clear and clean, and its little white slotted enamel label that told what time the letters would be collected. And indeed as Cassie, having loitered, stood there gazing on this unfamiliar object—for the post at home meant the small counter at the village shop and Bob Scase who delivered the letters—a man on a bicycle, blue-uniformed, wearing a peaked cap and trouser clips and carrying a sack over his shoulder, pulled neatly into the gutter. He propped his bike against the curb and came forward whistling and jingling a bunch of keys.

Cassie was taking a long time over dropping her letter into the box. She turned it in her hands, reading and re-reading the address as if such care might add some importance to the messages it carried. The postman stood back waiting for her, still whistling, his hat now a little tilted—until at last she dropped in the letter and heard its hollow fall among the rest. Because of a longing to see the little door in the pillar box opened, with all those secret letters and cards waiting inside to be speeded on their way, she did not turn away at once.

The postman crouched down on his hunkers by the pillar box, and reached into its belly with the friendly familiarity of a cowman helping out a calf from its mother. Without looking over his shoulder, he said cheerfully, "Haven't seen you before, have I?"

"You couldn't. Seeing I never see you," replied Cassie.

"Where you working?" he asked, for she had run out in the lace-trimmed cap and apron that Mrs. Garside had given her all neatly packed in a box.

"Have a guess," she said; and walked off at once,

thinking cheeky thing! but all the same feeling glad that he had bothered. A few houses on she could not help looking back, but he was already riding away, busy, intent on the next box on his round, his sack heavier than when he had spoken, full of jostling envelopes that held a thousand secrets—letters from wives to absent husbands, from girls to lovers; angry letters from parents to disappointing children, anxious ones from mothers to married daughters far away and expecting their first babies; bills; complaints. . . . All came from the houses Cassie passed, walking slowly, not wanting to go indoors from the scented, starry, dusty night. And she glanced as she went at the lighted windows, few with closed curtains, where people whose names she might one day know busied themselves about the time that lay between now and bed.

It was all so different from home it seemed a world of mystery. Although Dad had gone to London almost immediately his first wife died, he had never invited any one of his children to visit him. He had been the visitor, arriving almost shyly at Gran's, never precisely a stranger yet speaking already a little differently, his voice more like the voices Cassie had heard in the two weeks or so since she came back with him from his last visit. Then she had met her stepmother for the first time. The Garsides, of course, spoke in a posh manner, not as if they were trying to—like that girl who had come briefly to the village school—but as if they couldn't help it.

Cassie had reached the gate of No. 15 by now, and as the gate clicked she saw Mrs. Garside at the window, quite clearly looking out for her. She smiled and nodded, so that Cassie would know she was not being watched, just looked after. And indeed Cassie thought no other than this, yet bristled very slightly at being so clearly supervised.

She had to ring the front-door bell, and Mrs. Garside herself came to let her in.

"You may use the side door when you go to the post, Edith. Then you needn't ring."

Mrs. Garside made this sound like a favor, but Cassie immediately blushed furiously because she had done something wrong. Servants used side doors, of course they did. She should have thought of that, for they always went to the side doors of the big houses at home where any one of them—the village people, that is—happened to be working, or carrying some message. Perhaps Cassie had not expected No. 15 to rate as high as the manor or the Grange, but clearly Mrs. Garside thought differently. And it was her house after all.

"I should get off to bed now," Mrs. Garside said, when she had closed the front door.

"Just my sewing," Cassie murmured, "from out the kitchen."

"Good night, then."

"Good night, madam."

"Sleep well. The bed's quite comfortable, isn't it?"

"Oh yes, madam—thank you."

Cassie lowered her head. Her throat had lumped up dreadfully. Her slip over the front door burned inside her. She had sooner Mrs. Garside had spoken sharply, then she could have stiffened herself with a bit of temper. "When our Cassie spit," Gran always said, "she spit like a ten-headed tom."

The stairs were in front of Cassie. She forgot her sewing and bolted up them with her head down, blundering into her room. She sat down hard on the bed and loneliness hit her great crashing blows. She would have cried and bellowed, only here she must be private with her grief. She remembered Mr. Garside—his extraordinary job. If she told that to Gran, would she disapprove so much that Dad would fetch Cassie away and send her back to the only place where she truly belonged?

After a while, her grief easing into speculation, Cassie heard Miss Jean come springing up the stairs. Soon she was shut inside her own room. Mrs. Garside would not be coming up for some time; she always waited up for her husband, who came home very late. When she had turned her own light out and got into bed, Cassie could see under the cracks of the two doors that Miss Jean's light still burned. The thought of the older girl distracted Cassie from her own affairs. She lay awake briefly, wondering what Miss Jean was up to.

. . . Jean was writing in her enormous journal, which she had kept already for several years. Sometimes she thought she would tear out the early part, written while she was away at boarding school; she found it hopelessly immature. "Mother gets worried," she wrote, "because she thinks the girl will be lonely. Of course she will be lonely, sitting all by herself each evening without even a wireless. She is a country maid. She has come from a village with brothers and sisters and an old church and farms and things. If I could only learn about the country I could write a country book full of middens and pitchforks and poppies and corn. What a hope! I don't even know how many men work on a farm. Surely she could tell me that much? She's pretty, I think, dark hair, pink cheeks, brown eyes; small. ∴ . . Why can't I be small? Why must I have big feet? Perhaps everyone is lonely, really, only we don't like to think about it."

2

ON WEDNESDAY afternoons Cassie visited her father's home. It was about twenty minutes' walk away and she had soon learned the shortcuts through the side streets. These grew narrower and more modest as she neared Dad's place, till they were rows of low-pitched cottages, very neat, with tiny tidy gardens and joined together like seats in a cinema. The way at one point led through the quiet graveyard of an old church. There had been a village here once, but only the church, squat and crumbly, seemed to remember. On the top corner of the street beyond the church was a little shop, and certainly that was not unlike a village shop; only the customers were different. It was Dad's shop. Once, at home, he had been a farm laborer, stockman at the big farm up the street beyond the pub. Now he was a shopkeeper. It seemed extraordinary to Cassie; which was rather absurd, for she could not even remember him in those early days, since she had been barely four years old when her mother died.

The shop was shut on Wednesday afternoons, so Cassie used the side door. Today, as on other Wednesdays, the door was unlocked, she pushed it and went in, calling as she went.

"You home, then, Mum?"

Her stepmother was in the kitchen, doing some ironing. There was a smell of hot clothes, a hint of scorch.

"There you are, dear," Mrs. Martle said, smiling at Cassie. "And how's the world with you?"

"That Master Roddy pulled my knitting undone!"

Instead of sounding cross, Cassie sounded rather proud —as if the naughty clever boy were somehow hers.

Mrs. Martle clicked her teeth, saying, "There now! I hope he said he was sorry."

"Not till bedtime. . . . Madam say he'll have to go to boarding school. Ask me, he only need a spank now and then. But they're not spanking people."

"Well, you can be too hard. And you can be too soft. Put the kettle on, dear. I baked some of that gingerbread. Your dad'll be in soon. He just went to post off some orders. How's that Miss Jean you were on about last time?"

"All right."

"What's she do with herself all day?"

"Reads."

"Is that all?"

"She sit b'the hour in her own bedroom. Writing."

"Oh—that's it. Clever. I say, she's clever, is she?"

"No. Yes. I don't know," Cassie said.

They both laughed. They were very easy together.

This kitchen was somewhere in between Gran's kitchen and Cassie's kitchen, that is, Mrs. Garside's. It was bigger than one, smaller than the other. It was pin-clean. The linoleum was patterned and highly polished. There was a rag rug by the kitchen range. That, for sure, had been made by Cassie's sister, Margery, for she was making

18

them all the time. It looked nice, a piece of home. Cassie was more accustomed by now to being away from home. She thought of it longingly, but calmly.

"Our Marge made that rug," she stated—as if her stepmother did not know.

"That's true, she did. Did you write your gran, Cassie?"

Cassie nodded.

"Did she write back yet?"

"Her eyes don't let her."

"Never mind. One of the girls'll do it for her."

"Our Queenie will. But that take a long time."

Mum looked at Cassie and smiled, as if she knew but would not say. What she knew was that though Cassie was in her father's house she was only a visitor, and felt a visitor, and that her father was her father but she did not know him very well.

"There, dear," said Mum, "there's the kettle. You make the tea and I'll just see these things folded."

Presently Mr. Martle came home.

"Well, then—how's our girl?"

Cassie told again the sum of her news—Master Roddy and the knitting, Miss Jean and her reading. Mrs. Garside and her nice friendly manner. The feeling increased that they were hers, there was a small stir of pride in the Garsides—as if positions were reversed and it was she who employed them.

"It was a good day I stopped to look at them small ads," Mrs. Martle said. "You're a lucky girl to find such a good place. I say you're a lucky girl."

Cassie smiled. She felt pleased with herself for being a lucky girl, though it was none of her doing.

Yet when it was time to go back, she was reluctant. Dad took her into the shop, where the blinds were down, and found her some packets of chocolate and a tin of toffee.

"Keep you going till next time, eh?" he said. Then he slipped a pink sugar mouse into a paper bag. "Here—take that for the little lad."

He then walked with her to the corner of Stanton Avenue, where he said good night.

"Keep your pecker up," he said. "You know Mum and me's not far away. If anything goes wrong, there's the phone. The number's in the book—Martle's Stores. But nothing can," he added, firmly and a bit hastily, as if he was putting ideas into her head and offering her a chance she would take at the first opportunity.

Then he said, kissing her cheek quickly, mumbling, "Mum's very fond of you. Know that? She's very fond of you."

He was gone, and only a hundred yards or so separated Cassie Martle from her little room at No. 15.

Cassie went in by the side door that opened straight into the kitchen. The light was on. Miss Jean was there, ironing; just as Mum had been in the other kitchen. It seemed strange, somehow. It joined them up—though Mum had been ironing Dad's shirts and Miss Jean was ironing her cami-knickers, that were pink crepe de chine trimmed with a coffee-colored lace. She had made them herself, stitching for hours, embroidering on the lace. You might have thought she was making a trousseau. She looked up as Cassie came in and said, almost guiltily,

"I've practically finished." The iron whizzed up and

down. "I've let it get too dry," she said. "Damn." She frowned and looked furious.

"I'll roll them down," said Cassie. "They'll do in the morning." She knew she was going to say more and tried not to, but out it came. "I'll do them for you, if you like, miss."

"Oh, no" cried Miss Jean, all in a hurry. "I'm sure you haven't got the time. I'll do them—I'll do them. Well —you just roll them up for me—but I'll iron them." Then she said, "How were they?" As Cassie hesitated, she said, "I mean your father, and your—your. . . ."

"Quite well, thank you." She remembered what was in the bag with her sweets. She took out the sugar mouse and put in on the table. "That's for Master Roddy."

"Oh—oh, gosh! He'll love that! You are kind, Cassie."

"It was Dad."

"*Was* it? Oh, he'll love it!" She held the mouse on the palm of her hand and stroked it gently. "It's marvelous. It's absolutely marvelous!"

Just then Mrs. Garside came into the kitchen.

"There you are, Edith. Did you enjoy your day off?"

"Yes, Madam. Thank you."

"There's a letter for you. I put it in your room. Perhaps it's from home."

It was from home. Queenie had written on lined paper torn out of an exercise book. She was two years younger than Cassie, still at school.

"Dear Cass," Queenie had written, "I hope you are well. I write this for Gran, seeing she do not see. But that is, too, from me, the letter is. Saturday old Mrs. Billacre die and were buried Tues. Her daughter come from

Colchester and clean out the cottage like she were a mad thing. All was thrown out in the garden so Amy and me went looking I found a little card with daisies and *God is Love* Amy a buttonhook we took them home they were not wanted. Mr. S. up the church took sick at the service Sunday last and is better now. Katie had her baby a huge big boy. Leslie says to say What ho. No more news. Your loving sister Queenie."

Queenie always had a nose for deaths and such matters. It was lovely to have a letter, but there was nothing in it except Katie's baby that Cassie needed to know. Katie was Leslie's wife. She was always having babies, so that was nothing new, and Leslie always said, "What ho!"

Cassie sat on her bed with the letter in her hand. She read it several times, as if there must be something more that she had not noticed the time before. Gradually she heard Queenie's voice creeping through, even to the way she went on and on without pausing to take a breath. Then the little room filled up with remembered things. Cassie lay back on the pillow, holding the letter still, like a talisman, like a charm through which she saw and remembered, afraid to put it down.

Now that she was away from it she had begun to see home for what it was. When she was there she called it home, but that was only a word like any other, like hat or table. It was in fact the place from which she took all her being, that made her what she was, whatever that might be. She could feel this, but without finding any words. She had come a long way and wanted only to return, and took it for granted that she would return. It was like something learned in Sunday school—coming from God and returning to God—something that nobody could really be expected to think about. Home did seem as solemn as God to Cassie as she lay in the little room at the Garsides', the room that was called hers but which could never be so because here was not where she belonged.

Yet already, in the few weeks that she had been here, home had in part released her. She no longer felt that she needed to cry. Calmly and with pleasure she called home to her mind, counting over the many things about it that she had accepted without question and now considered lovingly. Not only Gran—but old Lizzie popping in from across the lane; and saying good morning to the vicar and pulling faces behind the back of Colonel Fielding, or Lady Gwen from the Grange—always so sweetly friendly but never remembering your name. She thought of the clipped lavender under the cottage windows, the vegetable patch when it was newly turned and ready for planting, her brother Jack coming in with a little packet of cabbage plants that a neighbor had given him; the lilac flowering; the stump of pear tree where the tree-creepers nested; the wild bees in the parlor chimney where a fire could never be lighted because it was good luck to have them there. . . . All this would be continuing, day by day and minute by minute, even though Cassie was not there to see and hear. It would not stay frozen in time without her, but if she needed it tomorrow, it would be there; and it would still be hers.

When Cassie got into bed properly, she took Queenie's letter with her, and slid it under the pillow.

But that was quite late. Miss Jean had come up and

had even put out her light. Mrs. Garside had come upstairs and, as she often did, gone down again in her dressing gown and slippers to wait for her husband's return. Cassie heard her moving about from the kitchen to the diningroom, then the key slid in the latch and Mr. Garside was home. Cassie listened to the rumble of his deep voice with pleasure, first in greeting, then in conversation with his wife, when she sat with him as he settled to his supper. No doubt he was telling her of the day's work, like any other returning husband. Only it was the evening's work, and of so strange a nature that Cassie had not yet come to accept it as a part of everyday life.

Mr. Garside was an actor—he was Miles Garside, whose name Cassie had seen printed in *The Radio Times*, whose voice she had actually heard coming over the air and out into his own sitting room. Cassie had seen the name, too, in a theater program lying about. The play he was appearing in at present had already been running for some time.

It was a truly amazing thing to Cassie that so ordinary a person in daily life should actually be paid to paint his face and dress up and strut about speaking words he had not even thought up for himself, pretending to be someone else. She had never been in a theater in her life, Gran knew them to be sinful places where anything might happen. She would never be able to tell Gran about Mr. Garside, that was sure. And that was a pity, for she could only admire him—tall, and dark, with that beautiful voice and just a hint of coming from some other world. He never left the house without kissing his wife good-bye, and he never returned without kissing her in greeting. For that matter, she never left the house, either, even if it was only to go to the shops, without saying good-bye properly. When Cassie came to think about this she realized that it was good practice—for what if some disaster struck and one or the other never returned? At least they would have said a kind good-bye. . . . This was the sort of thing Gran might have thought of, and it surprised Cassie to recall that she never had.

Compared with the fondness and patience of the parents the son and daughter seemed like strangers. The little boy was wicked, willful and high-spirited; his sister became increasingly hard for Cassie to understand. The scoldings and so on that resulted from Master Rodney's antics were reasonable enough—but the furious, bursting rages of Miss Jean, against one parent or the other, shocked Cassie to the depths. She had never spoken of them on her days off and she believed she never would. Miss Jean was nearest to her in age and so she felt a kind of obligation to her—she was bound to accept what she did. It would have been easiest to think of her as mad, only quite clearly she was no such thing. When things were going smoothly she and her mother seemed to be laughing all the time. And sometimes when she had been shut up in her room, writing and writing, she came out white-faced and with glittering eyes, swinging away down the stairs as though her feet no longer needed to touch the ground.

The more different Cassie felt from the Garsides, the more important they became to her. Their peculiarities solaced her loneliness. It was because of them that she began to grow self-sufficient, feeling a need to look after them and protect them.

Ten minutes away there was the common, and beyond that lay the park. The common suited Cassie, and there she took the little boy for walks. He was always looking out for his friend, Bruce Richardson. Bruce had a little sister, Philippa, who was wheeled in a pram by Elsie—the Richardsons' Cassie, you might say. Cassie and Elsie sat together on a bench beside the path, while the two boys roared and bellowed and banged one another about, or played quieter, more mysterious games among the gorse and the hawthorn, stalking one another, springing out silently, then bursting into banging and pointing of imaginary guns and falling about very realistically when one or the other had been shot dead. Young Rodney was better at this than Bruce; you could see he had acting in his blood.

"Little monkeys," said Elsie. She was fair where Cassie was dark, and she took great care with her eyebrows. The fuzzy fair ones had been plucked away and each morning and afternoon she drew a thin clever line with eyebrow pencil. She also wore a fair amount of powder and lipstick, which Mrs. Richardson, so Elsie told Cassie, did not much like. "But when it comes to faces, it's up to the person, I always say." She smiled at Cassie in a tolerant but friendly way. "I can see you're a country girl, all right. Like a mouse, aren't you? I can see I shall have to bring you out a bit." She was nineteen, so she seemed to Cassie quite old and bold. "What do you do, afternoons off?"

"I go to my dad's place."

"Wednesday's my day, too," said Elsie. "We could go up the West End by bus."

"I don't know what Mum would say. She expects me."

"Oh," said wise Elsie, "she'll be glad you've got a friend. And so will both the madams, you see if they don't. Mrs. R. thinks I only want to go out with boys."

"Don't you?"

"Enough's enough, if you know what I mean. Too jolly stuck on themselves, the most of 'em."

Cassie smiled and bit her lip, admiring bold Elsie. The idea of a trip to the very heart of London excited her. How would she wait until next Wednesday—today was only Friday.

"I'm off this Sunday, Elsie."

"Sunday's no more use than a sick headache. We want to look at the shops. Everything's dead as doornails on a Sunday. I'll meet you Wednesday."

Elsie was right. Both their ladies were glad they had found one another. Cassie could see that Mrs. Garside was really quite relieved, she knew her employer had worried about her and felt softly toward her—though she had made a fine old song and dance over two broken glasses only that morning. Life changed color for Cassie. Though Wednesday was a long way off it was bound to come.

"We're going on the bus to Oxford Street," she found herself telling Miss Jean; Jean was sitting at her writing table while Cassie dusted and swept the bedroom. "My friend Elsie say the shops are there."

"Oh yes, the shops are there all right. Mind you don't spend all your money."

"We'd never buy anything," said Cassie positively, knowing well that such places would be much too grand. "Not in the West End, we wouldn't."

"Have tea, then. Go to Lyons Corner House. Have tea and chocolate eclairs. And mind you don't get picked up."

When she had said it she went a little pink. Or perhaps what Cassie saw was merely a reflection of her own indignation. Picked up! What a common sort of way to talk! What would Gran say to that? Unwillingly, because it hurt strangely, Cassie thought of Ned Gooderham, and walking by the river, and the look he had given her when she said she was going away.

"Have you got a boy at home?" Miss Jean asked her.

"No, miss, I haven't," replied Cassie primly. "I don't think of it. I'm fully busy."

Miss Jean turned back to her scribbling, humming as she did so. "In this heart of mine You live all the time— Sweet Sue! Just you!"

On Wednesday at two o'clock Cassie had washed up the lunch things and changed and hurried to meet Elsie at the bus stop. Elsie was waiting for her. She looked very smart. Apart from her careful face, she was wearing a flowery dress very suited to the warm summer afternoon, white gloves, a white handbag and a floppy white hat. Cassie had seen no better hat at the vicarage fêtes at home. She herself was wearing the only summer dress she had, a plain blue cotton with a collar and cuffs of white spotted with blue and a white belt. Her hat was a round burnt straw with a navy blue ribbon. She looked at Elsie and felt very humble, and she could not fail to know that Elsie looked at her and was satisfied with her own appearance. Not that she showed it in any way, greeting Cassie with a loud welcoming cry.

"Here you are, then! All ready to see the sights!"

She made it sound so much more than pleasurable—adventurous, daring, even dangerous.

"Where shall we go, Elsie?"

"We can go all the way on the bus to Marble Arch. That'll be tenpence, Cassie. Have you got the money? I have if you haven't, so don't worry."

"I have," said Cassie. "Thanks all the same." It was good to have a kind and generous friend.

There was a bus coming toward them, and two others waiting at the stop moved forward and held up their hands.

"Not that one!" Elsie slapped down Cassie's rising hand. "Wait for a pirate—they go much faster."

This was a mystery to Cassie, but Elsie enjoyed explaining. Private companies ran buses to rival the red buses of the London Passenger Transport Board, stretching themselves to shorten the journey and so attract customers from the stodgier ride. They barely stopped, however, and when one arrived Elsie and Cassie had to spring and grab and clutch to scramble aboard, with difficulty and danger hauling themselves up the open top deck.

"In the front!" screeched Elsie, excited by the contest. The bus was already a quarter of a mile from the stop, swaying and jerking, intent on passing the red bus ahead, and achieving it to shouts from both drivers. The two girls clung on to the backs of the seats, bracing themselves, laughing helplessly as they were thrown from side to side by the dashing and triumphant skill of the driver, hanging on to their handbags and their hats as they struggled toward the prize of the two front seats, tripping over their own feet as they finally reached their goal.

It was a grandstand view provided they did not lose their hats. They hung on, breathless and laughing still, lurching against one another as the race continued, on along the main road with the shops, out at the far end into quieter waters, the houses standing back in well-kept gardens, roses bursting in the sun, scrambling and flocking over walls and porches. The girls looked down from the high poop of their pirate vessel, seeing not only flowers but children playing, perambulators standing by open doors, dogs stretched out on striped lawns, summer houses and deckchairs and swinging, cushioned seats under canvas awning. Then they were passing tennis courts, stopping at the last moment to pick up passengers. Chalky white figures moved in a loose pattern on the green grass courts—not very urgent, not very skilled, playing suburban afternoon tennis with pleasure and no hard feelings.

"Does that Miss Jean of yours belong to the tennis club?"

"It's not the kind of thing she like."

"What *does* she like?"

"Reading, mostly. And she write for hours."

"Poor thing," said Elsie.

They crossed the common, another common, that Cassie did not know. Now the bus was full and it seemed as if everyone must be going the same way, for no one pulled the cord on the step below, or banged on the lever by the stairs that rang the bell. Freed of all restraint, the pirate vessel careered along as if a thousand dolphins swam ahead to power it on its voyage.

"People always get off this side the river," Elsie said, knowing even where complete strangers alighted to seek their homes. "He's bound to stop there."

So indeed he did, but not for long, spewing forth passengers like bilge water, then dashing on.

Then for a time the best was over. They came to sad streets without order or beauty, where garages and small greengrocers jostled pawnshops with the sign of the three golden balls swinging above their doors. The bus charged ahead, though constantly balked by increasing traffic. The scene changed again, the street suddenly immensely widening, with houses in elegant terraces and crescents and smart motor cars. Then suddenly—The Shops!

"Is it the West End?" Cassie asked, using the expression for only the second time out loud, but hearing it as if it were a piece of a foreign language.

"It's Kensington High," said Elsie; and that sounded foreign, too.

"Let's get off, Elsie! Look at all the shops!"

"They're better in Oxford Street—and more of them. Anyway, we've paid our fare."

It was not yet three o'clock when their pirate set them

down at Marble Arch and sailed on its way. For a moment the pavement seemed to be moving and Cassie clutched at Elsie. She was stunned by the journey, by the magnificence of those palace-like dwellings that had appeared after the first shops, at the green expanses of the park, which they faced as if scorning to look upon any neighbor, at the crowds, sauntering in Park Lane, bustling in Oxford Street. Cassie had never seen so many people all at once, nor any human form so imposing and immense as that of the great bronze warrior standing under the trees by the entrance to the park with shield and sword at the ready.

Cassie had burst out with the first thing that came into her head. "Is it Big Ben?"

Elsie broke into wild laughter, recovering briefly to cry, "Big Ben's a *clock!*" and then collapsing again. . . .

But now Cassie had forgotten the feeling of humiliation, the smiles from strangers who had overheard, who perhaps felt their faces cracking into that strange infection of laughter that may capture any company and most of all on a summer day.

For the rest of that afternoon, in the company of thousands, the two girls walked and walked, passing slowly from shop window to shop window, eyeing the splendors, Elsie considering and critical, forever on the point of darting inside to buy, Cassie wide-eyed, hardly able to credit what she was seeing. Like a child at a frosty windowpane she almost pressed her nose against the glass that withheld the treasure from the gaping, envious crowd. Above evening dresses barely to the knee, the faces of the wax models gazed out in long-lashed insolence, their hands elegantly poised, inviting admiration. In neighbor windows others, more sporting, in tweeds and pull-on hats that hid their eyebrows, stood in brown brogues among tufts of artificial heather. *This autumn on the moors*, a card proclaimed in curly lettering.

"That means shooting," she told Elsie, glad of this modest bit of knowledge.

"As if I didn't know," said Elsie.

The heather touched Cassie strangely. Though she saw none of it in her part of the country, the Colonel went north at such times of the year and returned with bunches of the stuff on the bonnet of his big high Daimler. A surge of longing took Cassie, the vision in the window blurred, the glory vanished. Suddenly there was nothing around her but noise, heat and shoving, dusty, sweating shoppers.

The pavement now seemed red-hot, her shoes pinched.

"They're too heavy for this job," Elsie said. "We're not in the country now, you know. You need something lighter."

She led Cassie on to an enormous shoe shop and once more they stood staring. There seemed to be thousands of different shoes, high heels, ankle straps, dainty buckles, bedroom slippers with no back and bursts of feathery trimming, evening shoes in colored satin, gold shoes and silver. It was like some temptation arranged by a chairman and board of demons, and the shoes themselves, that should have been walking, running, dancing, were held imprisoned, waiting for the tempted to release them.

"Shall we have tea soon?" asked Cassie, a shade timidly, tired now and dispirited. "Miss Jean said Lyons Corner House."

"Oh, she did? Fuller's is better."

"But is it expensive?"

"The tea's my treat," Elsie said graciously.

But when they looked inside Fuller's it was all white table cloths and silvery teapots, high-nosed waitresses and smart hats.

"Lyons, then, Cassie."

They traipsed on along the less interesting side of the street, where it was a bit shady. Cassie now concentrated on the business of walking carefully, so that the least misery was endured, wishing that Elsie would suggest getting on a bus, but not knowing how far away Lyons was, not knowing if a bus would be worthwhile.

"Poor Cassie," said Elsie, taking her by the arm, losing all her lofty manner, sounding kind and understanding. "Let's pop in the first place we see. We can go to the Corner House any old time."

Later, fortified by tea and buttered toast and cream buns, they had to wait a long time for a bus to take them home—it had to be a pirate of the same kind as before, since they had taken a return ticket to save themselves a penny each way. At last it came swaying and gallant into sight, and they fought through a great battling crowd to get aboard.

"Inside only!" shouted the conductor, swinging like Douglas Fairbanks from the step.

They had to sit where they could, one at either end inside, stuffy and crowded and heavy with petrol fumes. Cassie was squeezed against the window by an enormous woman carrying two full shopping baskets, and Elsie was right up in front with only a small piece of seat to perch on, sharing with a young woman whose child, supposedly on its mother's knee, spilled its dusty feet onto Elsie's summer dress.

With the heat and the fumes and the swaying of the bus, Cassie began to feel sick. The journey home seemed much longer and she tried to distract herself by reading the advertisements that covered every suitable surface. They were all of the same product, and it was unfortunate that the product should be sardines. This was no moment for Cassie to dwell on such things but her eye could not escape their presentation—sardines lay oil-drenched and plump in their open tins, or were served for supper to delighted families of four. . . .

At last the bus came back to the spot from which the two girls had set out. By that time they had been able to move to a seat together.

"Have you enjoyed yourself, Cassie?" Elsie sounded the least bit anxious.

"Oh, *yes!*" answered Cassie fervently.

"See you on the common tomorrow, then."

Elsie would go on to the next stop, but Cassie left the bus and had only to totter down Stanton Avenue. Today it was like coming home. Home was the place where you could take your shoes off.

3

"CASSIE HAS grown very chummy with the Richardsons' Elsie," Jean wrote.

Now it was July. It was hot. Jean sat at her open window and stared as much at the view as at the page before her. A terrible thing was happening. The orchards beyond the garden fence were being cleared for the next row of new houses. One after the other, heavy with tiny apples that would never grow bigger, the trees went down like troops before an advancing enemy of superior force— like guns against bows and arrows. When the houses were up there would be another deprivation—the distant railway line would no longer be visible. At night the steam trains ran toy-size through the dark, smoke and flame gushing like some fantastic mane. The trains hooted at the level crossing and again as they approached the more distant station. The lovely melancholy was matched at times by small boats moving up river and passing slowly under the new bridge, still under construction.

A great gloom filled Jean. Nothing pleased her much at this moment of her life. Since her early school days she had intended to make her name in the theater; she would be a third generation. But as she had grown tall, she had grown shy. She would have preferred now to give in, to state her intention of becoming a writer. She felt unable to admit defeat, so that much humiliating time was spent interviewing managers who seemed to her to take one quick embarrassed look before saying there was really nothing at the moment. She would set out looking smart for a ten-o'clock appointment and return feeling and even looking somehow dusty. Her father, being set in a somewhat old-fashioned mold of acting, scoffed at drama schools; experience was the only training. Anyway, he was only moderately successfully, a working actor who would never be quite a star, so how could he have afforded the fees? As for becoming a writer, she knew no training for that save living, and how was that set in motion?

"Cassie is getting rather smart," Jean continued, turning in despair from the falling trees. "She has bought two hats lately and a pale blue coat and skirt. Mother thinks she is frittering her money away and tries to advise her how best to plan this great sum she earns. 'You should save a little each week, Edith, so that you'll have enough to pay the fare home when you have your holiday.' Cassie shuts her mouth tight and looks away. Mother is quite decent in saying this, for she must feel—I do— that if Cassie/Edith goes home for a fortnight she may never come back."

Cassie had thought of this, too. The hot weather brought back some of her loneliness. As she sat by herself in the evenings, reading now the books that Elsie lent her, the clock had never ticked so furiously. She thought of walking by the river through such summer evenings, grain long set in the ear, greenish-gold, the poppies now drooping, all the talk of harvest promise. She counted her money. Madam was right—she should have been content with one new hat. She became discontented, huffing and sighing for days on end, even sharp with young Roddy. Not that he seemed to mind, he was too busy about his own shouting concerns. The school holidays released him and his friend Bruce to roar and bang about in one family's garden or the other. Even Miss Jean, Cassie noticed, grew fed up with them. Usually she was very patient and spent hours of her time reading to them or inventing games, or finding clothes for them to dress up in so that they could give entertainments to their admiring parents. She made up their faces for them—made bandit mustaches, Chinaman pigtails of plaited black knitting wool, tea-cosy hats.

Some of these summer days Cassie made a picnic tea and so did Elsie. They met on the common with the children in their charge, sitting on mackintoshes on the grass in the shade of birch and hawthorn, pulling long grasses to chew and talking about life. Elsie discussed life more than Cassie, who felt that she knew very little about it. But she was an eager listener so she would learn.

"Miss Jean's going to be in a play," Cassie told Elsie one afternoon as she poured tea from a Thermos into kitchen cups. She had been bursting with the news ever since she stepped out from No. 15, but she had waited for the right moment. "You just wait a bit, Master Roddy. *I'll* undo the sandwiches."

"Going to play a part, you mean? Go on! Mrs. Richardson says she'll never be any good with that height and her big face."

"Well, we don't all know everything, do we?" said Cassie quietly. "She come home yesterday and tell Madam. I've got a walk-on, she say. I'm a Roman matron."

"What's that mean?"

"Shakespeare." Cassie had only recently heard about Shakespeare and felt glad of Elsie's apparent ignorance.

"Oh that," said Elsie. "You get it a lot on the wireless. Mr. Richardson likes it. Mrs. doesn't."

"Julius Caesar," said Cassie, getting into her stride. "At the Queen's Theatre, that is. Which is nice, seeing *he's* at the Globe. They're all but next door," she explained as Elsie looked pleasingly at sea. "That mean they can come home together at night."

"She's glad, is she?"

"Yes."

You might more properly say she seemed reborn. Cassie would not have been able to explain to Elsie the change that had come over Jean since she rushed home with her news. She had bounded into the kitchen half an hour later, not only to tell the tale again but to offer Cassie a blue jumper she had knitted for herself and had made too small.

"She has to go to rehearsals, Elsie. From next Monday. Three weeks."

"Will she be paid?"

"Well—for the play, she will. That's what they do it for, isn't it? Like work. Like a job. I don't suppose for rehearsals. . . ." Cassie had heard Miss Jean tell her mother how much, and it seemed a fortune. At first she thought she would not tell Elsie, but she could not resist being in the know. "Three pound a week," she said.

"Three pound! Just for that? Just for dressing up? Well, I don't know! Some people get all the luck."

"It isn't as if she get her keep, though, Elsie."

"We could go to a matinee, Cass, and see what she looks like."

The idea seemed at once alluring and impertinent to Cassie. But what was to stop them? Yes, she said; they could do that. It would be a chance to wear her pale blue.

The jam sandwiches and the Bovril sandwiches were being shared out. Roddy had stamped on a bag of buns and Bruce had sent an uncorked Thermos flying, so there would be no second cups. Now the boys were slowly wrestling a few yards away on the grass, intent, it seemed, on exterminating one another as painfully and lingeringly as possible.

"I forgot to say, Cassie—I met a nice boy at the dance up the church hall Saturday."

"Go on."

"Alan. Fair. Topping dancer."

"Tall?"

Why had she asked the one undesirable question?

"Broad, rather," Elsie said carefully. "Anyway—there's another hop two Saturdays on. You could come."

"I haven't got the right dress."

"What'd I say? I said you'd have to get a dress. Didn't I? Didn't I say that weeks ago? It's the Sales starting next week. We'll go to Selfridge's on Wednesday and you can get yourself something."

"I haven't got anyone to go with. I haven't got a partner. I can't just do dancing without I've got a boy to go with." Cassie had learned this much of a world wider than her own—at home there was none of this formality.

"Alan'll bring his pal, Len. He said he would, so you needn't look so stuck up. Who d'you think you are?"

"Saturday . . . I'd have to ask Madam."

"Ask her when you get back today."

"I never had a Saturday yet. It's not my day. I never asked any different."

"Got to be a first time, hasn't there?"

It took Cassie a day or two to approach Mrs. Garside. When she did so the effect was far different from any she had expected. Mrs. Garside was instantly anxious, anxious not to stop Cassie's fun, anxious not to be a spoilsport— and anxious in another way.

"You don't know anything about Elsie's friends, do you? Who are these young men who want to go with you?"

"We shall buy our own tickets, madam." Cassie thought this must surely make the whole thing decent. "That's at the *church* hall," she said, anxious in her turn, beginning to see the dance slipping away and with it the excuse to buy a dress.

"Yes, of course, Edith, I'm sure I'm fussing. But while you're in this house you're in my care. You do see, don't you? I am responsible for you to your father. What would he think if I let you go out with some unsuitable stranger?"

"I don't know," Cassie said. And she really did not know, for at home there seemed only girls and boys and never one unsuitable stranger. Most girls had been at school with the boys they eventually married—there just were no strangers. Some were wild and some were wicked, but they all settled down in the end. She must have looked very crestfallen, for Mrs. Garside said quickly that she would telephone Mrs. Richardson and see what she thought.

"I'm just taking care of you, my dear."

This, too, had a curious effect on Cassie. Her feelings about the Garsides were in a constant state of change. First she had been wary, then she had grown possessive. Now there was something different again. As she turned back into the kitchen to set about the washing-up her eyes had filled with the old familiar tears. Or were they so familiar? They were not tears of loneliness or resentment or even disappointment, for Mrs. Richardson was younger than Mrs. Garside and therefore had more sense, so the dance was still well within reach. What moved Cassie was discovering that Mrs. Garside considered her in this way—as a care and a responsibility. It was as if Cassie had been shifted several moves on a board marked out with a family game, in which she found she had unexpected claims. A bit like sharing an umbrella with Miss Jean, Cassie thought—then giggled rather painfully at the image. She came to her senses, thinking more sharply, as she knew Elsie would think, Cinderella and one of the Ugly Sisters, more like. . . . Not that Miss Jean was ugly, exactly—more what Gran called homely. Yet not quite that, either, because of some cleverness that lit her sharply at times.

As she dried the dishes, Cassie heard Mrs. Garside telephoning Mrs. Richardson.

"Oh well," she said, "in that case. . . ."

At that moment the grocer's boy came to the kitchen door. The rest of the conversation was lost in a sharp, pert exchange between the pair of them as Cassie unpacked the groceries.

"Mind and don't leave the gate swinging," she said, as she handed back the empty basket.

"Mind and don't leave the gate swinging," he mimicked as he moved away from the passageway between No. 15 and No. 13, banging the gate in the wall and taking care that it swung back gaping.

"Well, there you are, Edith," Mrs. Garside was saying cheerfully, putting her head round the kitchen door. "Mrs. Richardson is quite happy about the dance, so I shall be, too."

Once the arrangement had been made the time had seemed endless between now and then. But eventually Cassie found herself, trembling slightly, entering the hall with Elsie, wearing the pink marocain dress they had chosen for her between them, and new shoes to go with it. And a beige handbag Elsie had persuaded her to buy, though her money was running out and she had to be lent the extra five shillings. Being in debt was as good as a sin, but it was only till the end of the week and the bag put the finishing touch. They had bought it at Swan and Edgar's.

"Not much like the palais," Elsie said as they stepped inside the church hall, a converted army hut painted a kind of green. It was a warm night and they had no coats for the cloakroom, though some giggling girls were there, changing their shoes.

Truly it was a very dreary little hall, but someone had done his best by slinging festoons of colored lights web-like under the ceiling, and the musicians, piano, saxophone and bass, perched on the six-inch-high platform among pots of borrowed geraniums and trails of ivy.

"There was a crooner last time," Elsie said. "A redhead in a skimpy dress. I suppose the vicar was shocked." Then she let out a mild shriek. "There's Alan! That must be Len!" There was a pause before she added, sounding as if she thought she might have made her own choice too soon, "He's taller."

The boys wore their good dark suits and the meeting between the four was a shade constrained. If Elsie liked the look of Len, Cassie found herself purloined by Alan and it was in the reverse order that they first took the floor.

"Elsie tells me you're from the country," Alan said as, rising to his feet in a swooping kind of way, he swept Cassie off. "So what do you think of London, *mademoiselle?*"

"Oh—nice," replied Cassie, giggling at the *mademoiselle*, wanting to call him *monsieur*, which she knew was right because it was the only French word she knew, but afraid to bring it out in case it sounded wrong.

Though Alan was not as tall as Elsie would have liked, he contrived in some fashion to tower over Cassie. His hair was brushed into a bit of a quiff and neatly Brylcreemed. As soon as he began to dance he flashed his teeth dramatically. He danced with his shoulders high and his grip was near torture. As he swept round the floor in a spectacular foxtrot it must have been plain to anyone watching that there was only one dancer in the pair, for

Cassie's feet were barely permitted to touch the ground, and she was held in such a clamp against his firm torso that she could hardly breathe, her physical discomfort increased by her acute embarrassment.

The dance concluded to scattered applause, the evening being young and the hall no more than half full. Elsie and Len were approaching from the far side of the hall. Elsie looked disgruntled and was fanning herself with her handkerchief.

"Poor old Len—not much of a dancer," Alan said in Cassie's ear. "Now your friend Elsie!" He kissed his fingertips in a foreign way. "The cat's pajamas!"

As he spoke he gave Cassie a sharp slap on the bottom. This final display of total masculinity ended their relationship as far as Cassie was concerned. She wished she had not come. Mrs. Garside had been right; a girl needed to be careful.

"Shall we?" asked Len, when the other two rose smartly for the next dance, and were off before Cassie knew what was happening. The band had started up a medley announced as "Tunes of Yesteryear" and the pianist soon began singing as he played. "Yesteryear" struck Cassie as a silly way to describe tunes that her brother Jack still played happily on his portable gramophone, winding it with enthusiasm and always ready for one more. "The Sheik of Araby," "Tea for Two," "Last Night on the Back Porch," "K-k-k-katie," "I Want to be Happy," "Dinah." . . . "Shall we?" asked Len again, clearing his throat.

He held her diffidently and she saw at once that this excursion could well be as disastrous as her last. He looked anxious, concentrated. His brownish hair fell over one blue eye so that she could hardly see it, which gave him a strangely intense expression. He was a good deal taller than Alan, but she felt quite easy with him, since there was none of that leaning from the waist that she had found so awkward. He appeared a little afraid to pick up his feet, but he knew some steps and as long as he took them in strict rotation he managed all right, and she soon learned what to expect. He was silent, probably counting, and she found nothing to say. From time to time she caught a glimpse of Elsie and Alan giving what amounted to an exhibition one-step. The rest of the dancers began gradually to leave the pair more and more room, until at last there were only two other couples prepared to compete. Then they, too, gave up. The band stepped up the pace but the pair did not falter and when the music finally drew to a long concluding chord, there was a lot of clapping and stamping and calling out.

"Thanks," Cassie said politely to Len, as they returned to their seats after watching the last detail of this performance.

"Shall we have the next?" he asked, shoving back his hair from his damp forehead, suddenly revealing his second eye and giving her a confiding smile. "My sister's been teaching me," he said. "Of course I'm not up to old Alan."

"Nor I'm not up to old Elsie!"

Laughing happily at their own wit, they sat down side by side and wondered what next they should say to one another.

"Did you enjoy the dance?" Miss Jean came asking

next morning. "What about Elsie's young man—what's his name?"

"Alan."

"Did you dance with him?"

"Once was enough."

"Oh dear. . . ."

"I dance with Len, Miss Jean. That's the friend Alan brought. Len Eversley."

"Often?"

"Fairly often." Very slightly, Cassie tossed her head. "Not the Charleston, though!" She could not help laughing to recall the Charleston. "We're not let dance that in our village hall. The rector he call it a heathen dance."

"Oh well—once upon a time the waltz was thought most improper."

"Oh never! Oh it couldn't've!"

"It jolly well was. Then it was danced at the Duchess of Richmond's ball on the eve of Waterloo," Miss Jean said, not as if she meant to instruct Cassie but as if it gave her pleasure to speak of this thing. Cassie had no idea what she was talking about. Richmond was just down the road and Waterloo was a railway station. "There came a sound of revelry by night. . . . Well, I'm glad you enjoyed it." Miss Jean paused at the door. "What does your Len do when he's at home?"

"Do you mean his job?"

"Yes—what's his job?"

"He's learning to be a bus conductor," Cassie said, feeling pride and pleasure in her turn.

"No! What a wonderful thing to be! I never thought I'd know a girl who danced with a man who's going to be a bus conductor!" And she burst into the song that went, "I've danced with a man Who's danced with a girl Who danced with the Prince of Wales."

Cassie reddened a bit, wondering now if this might be mockery.

"You wait till you tell Roddy, Cassie. He's bound to want to be a bus conductor or a bus driver. Mind you keep in with Len, then when the time comes he can use his influence and get Roddy a job."

That time she really did go off, singing again about the Prince of Wales. Cassie was left with what she had had no chance to tell—that Len had blue eyes and brown hair, a bit curly, and that he was a lot taller than Elsie's Alan. It would be foolish to pretend, however, that he was anything like the heroes in the paper-covered romances Elsie lent her. Those were either alarmingly passionate or humiliatingly taciturn. Len was nowhere, in comparison. Besides, he was by no means the first boy Cassie had encountered. She had grown up with brothers and brothers' friends. And there was Ned. She was well able to wait and see whether Len would reappear.

It simply did not occur to Cassie that she might not marry and get a home of her own. It would occur more to Miss Jean, who seemed to have few friends, and those all girls, and who had never once, since Cassie came to No. 15, gone out dancing, or to any party that sounded at all exciting. She led a very strange life indeed, when Cassie came to consider it. She was simply not the sort of girl men would get excited about. What it really amounted to was that Cassie was pretty enough to attract attention and Miss Jean was not. In a world where girls were far too plentiful it stood to reason that the pretty ones would manage best.

"First night tomorrow," was all that Jean had time to write in her journal the whole of that week. . . .

Cassie was in bed but not asleep when Miles Garside and his daughter got home that night. She had been thinking about Miss Jean all the evening, and could not sleep for wondering how the play had gone. Mrs. Garside had seemed excited, too, though she had not gone to the first night of *Julius Caesar* by William Shakespeare at the Globe Theatre; Cassie was growing accustomed to these strange words, so far from what she had been likely to use until now. Mrs. Garside had set about a special sort of supper in honor of the occasion—Cassie was always amazed at how much Mr. Garside was able to eat at midnight. His play ended at eleven, and then he had to get his make-up off and travel home by tube and bus. Usually his key turned in the lock at about ten minutes past twelve, but tonight he was a bit later, because of meeting his daughter at her own stage door. Indeed, Cassie clearly heard him say, "Sorry to be so late, my dear." She pictured him sweeping off his hat and stooping to kiss her as usual.

"How did it go?" Mrs. Garside asked, as she carried the tray through into the dining room.

Cassie stretched out her arm and silently opened her door a foot or so.

"Marvelous! Marvelous!" cried Miss Jean, very excited. "Oh, it was marvelous!"

"Give it four weeks," Mr. Garside said.

They went into the dining room as Miss Jean replied, her voice higher than before. Mrs. Garside said something but it was a bit too late. The voices rose, though Cassie could no longer hear the words. Then again she spoke and they calmed down, and for a bit all went well. It was rather like hearing a play on the wireless, carrying on in some distant room. Both Mr. Garside and Miss Jean spoke in loud, dramatic voices at the best of times— which was reasonable enough. In fact it was almost the only thing about them that suggested they were anything other than ordinary respectable people.

Then quite suddenly the whole thing blew up. Miss Jean said something. Her father replied. He laughed. Mrs. Garside, barely heard, her voice was so soft by comparison, spoke quickly. This time it was no good. Cassie bit her fingers as she listened. Mr. Garside's voice became huge. She could almost hear what he was saying, only by that time she did not want to. She was on Miss Jean's side now, though in earlier days when she heard them quarreling she had not been so sure. She felt the tide of excitement on which the other girl had come home—just as Cassie herself had come home from the dance in the church hall—and the anguish now as everything was for some reason swept away. . . .

Eventually the dining-room door was flung open and wildly slammed. The little house shook to the fury of it. Noisily crying, Miss Jean rushed upstairs and flung into her own room. There was some slight movement from her brother's room at the racket, but then he slept again. Below her in the dining room Cassie heard husband and wife, she very quiet, he answering with tremendous emphasis and intensity. . . .

Cassie lay in her bed, stiff and distressed. Her door was now closed. The rags and ruins of the evening seemed to possess her, too.

Jean scribbled madly: "It's his vanity. He knows he's a wonderful Antony and he cannot bear anybody else playing it. He wants *Caesar* to fail because he's not in it." She read this and then inked it all out. She did so reluctantly. But she was writing for posterity which might think harshly of a daughter writing of her father in this vein. She rushed on, all the same, aching for relief, "Why did I tell him what I told him? I thought he'd be pleased. . . ."

As she sat with him and her mother over supper she had blurted, "Charles Marston said I looked beautiful."

Her father laughed. He had a big full laugh that was in fact one of his charms, only it was not charming to her then.

"I shouldn't take too much notice of remarks like that, my dear," he said.

Elsie had wanted Cassie to ask Jean if she would get them free tickets for a Wednesday matinee.

"She couldn't. She's not important. She hasn't words to say—she tell me so. She's not like Mr. Garside. He could."

"Well, ask him, then. We'll go to his play another Wednesday."

"I'll see," said Cassie.

Now they stood in a queue for the gallery—1/3. It had

been a race to get there on time, as Cassie had not wanted to say where she was going—Mrs. Garside would have let her go off earlier if she had. However, the queue was small and when they got into the theater it was plain that the place would be pretty empty.

The stairs to the gallery were stone and noisy, and the gallery seats were wooden benches. There was a great thumping on the boards as the few who had waited outside rushed for the best places. But in the rest of the theater there was a muffled quiet. Program sellers, in blue dresses and little frilly aprons with caps to match, stood counting out change into bags slung on their wrists. Cassie, who had never been inside a theater before, looked down rather sickly from the front row of the gallery. It was the second tier in this theater, but Elsie, who knew about such matters, said that in some theaters there were three.

"There's the dress circle—that's where they wear evening dress when it's not a matinee—and then the upper circle and then the gallery. The upper circle's at the back of the dress circle here, so you can't see it. Downstairs it's the stalls and the pit. You have to queue for the pit, like you do for the gallery, and you can wear ordinary clothes. Then there's the stalls, which are posh, and the boxes. Those are for the real nobs. Sometimes the King and Queen go to the theater. They go in a box."

"It's proper stuffy," said Cassie. She looked around her at the doors with EXIT above them in red lighted letters. They were lit by gas and you could see the little fan-shaped flame flickering away. Cassie marked the best way out in case she felt faint. She had never felt faint in her

52

life, but the airlessness and the height and her excitement made anything seem possible. "How long till it starts?"

"Nearly half an hour."

"There's nobody coming.

"We're Early Doors. I told you—it's all bookable except where you can see people sitting now. There's no need for them others to come in till the last minute."

Gradually, far below, a few people trickled in. In the dress circle, half of which they could see, they were mostly women. But in the stalls there were men as well, of a superior sort who, Elsie said, never had to go to work, but sauntered about the town, popping into their clubs, reading *The Times*, pausing by the flower sellers in Piccadilly Circus and buying a carnation for their buttonhole. One by one seats were tipped down, with discreet little thuds or clumsy crashes. The program girls moved along the rows, showing people where to sit, selling programs and boxes of chocolates, now groping for change in the little bags hanging in readiness from the left wrist, scribbling down the numbers of seats whose occupiers would like tea brought to them on a tray in the first interval or the second.

Cassie became aware of movement, too, in the area between the front row of the stalls and the stage itself. The orchestra was settling in, the players' movements faintly seen under a roofing of artificial palm branches. In the center there was a gap and there in due course the head and arms of the orchestra's conductor appeared like a jack-in-the-box.

"There!" said Elsie, suddenly losing her calm sophistication and clutching Cassie's arm.

The curtains had been pulled, rattling their rings across the exit doors. The conductor raised his baton. The music began. It suggested much conflict ahead. It was foreboding and heavy with a lot of drum. Then, just as the suspense began to seem unbearable, the music too boring to endure, the red velvet, gold-fringed curtains rose. All life, all time shifted and became another universe.

Cassie and Elsie would never claim that they had enjoyed the play; rather, they enjoyed themselves in spite of it. The words were hard to understand, the situations curious, the men appeared demented and the women were few. It was exciting when they all stabbed Caesar, even though Elsie quickly explained that the daggers were made of wood or even rubber, while the blood was most likely tomato ketchup. She was shushed by a stringy young man in spectacles who was reading the whole thing in a book, hanging over the edge of the gallery to catch some light from the stage at which he barely glanced. . . . Then it was the interval and the tea trays for the privileged. . . .

Cassie was quite silent in the interval. The sight of Miss Jean, moving among a crowd of others, difficult to spot at first and then recognized with a thrill of pride, was all that Cassie asked of this occasion. She could hardly believe the tall dignified figure, draped in a long flowing crimson garment which she handled with a sweeping grace, could really be Jean Garside who scribbled and wept in the next bedroom at No. 15.

"Tell you what," Elsie said, just before the lights went down for the second act.

"What?"

"I think she looks lovely."

"She look beautiful, Elsie."

For a second Elsie considered. Then she nodded. "That's right. Beautiful."

The lights were down. The curtain rose. There she was calling out among a great mob of others. . . .

It was more than a week before Cassie could bring herself to speak of having witnessed a matinee performance of *Julius Caesar* by William Shakespeare. Then Miss Jean came into the kitchen on her usual quest for the iron. Over her arm was an evening dress that Cassie had seen her wear once or twice to go with her mother to a theater. The dress was pale green. It had beads all over it. If a thread got broken the beads fell off; Cassie was forever sweeping them up off the bedroom carpet.

"I'm out of work," Miss Jean said, pulling a face as she got out the iron. "Notice is up."

"What's that, miss?"

"It means they've pinned a piece of paper on the notice board at the stage door. It says the run will be concluded next Saturday."

Miss Jean shook out the dress and a tiny bead or two pattered on the kitchen linoleum. She seemed excited as well as gloomy. "One of the men is having a party after the theater tonight. He's asked about fifteen people. Supper and dancing. It's at a night club called The Gargoyle. I shan't be coming home. I'm staying with one of the other girls."

"Is that the one you stand with when the man's talking?" Cassie asked, without stopping to think. Then she turned her usual bright pink as Miss Jean stared at her.

"Have you *seen* it? Do you mean you went to *see* it?"

"Elsie and me went. We went to a matinee—in the afternoon. I never got to a theater before. That was a surprise."

"Well? Well—what did you think?"

"We spotted you."

"Oh—good."

"We both sit there and say the same thing, Miss Jean. She look beautiful. Both said."

Miss Jean began to smile, and then seemed to remember something.

"That was a surprise, too!"

"Oh it was, miss!"

She realized and bit her lip, turning from pink to a less becoming shade.

Jean laughed. Then she said, "Well, thanks, Cassie. I'll take it as a compliment, both ways round."

4

"TOO FAST the summer goes over," Jean wrote; then crossed it out and wrote instead, "Summer is almost over." She sighed after distinction and could not find it.

However it was expressed, the season began to look jaded—roses dropped, the scent of the neighbors' honeysuckle climbed through Cassie's window. Gypsy women with baskets strolled these quiet dull streets, crying, "Sweet lavender."

"The end of the summer," Mrs. Garside said to Cassie. The strangely harsh cry, half song, half shout, drifted and echoed, remaining in the ear and in the heart long after its melancholy was drawn away into the distance. No wonder Mrs. Garside gave a sigh, gazing from the open window as if she saw her life being dragged away, too.

Cassie thought, I didn't know she. . . . But then she lost the thought, unable to name what it was she was trying to comprehend. . . .

Cassie was not to go home after all. She would spend her holiday with her father and stepmother, but Queenie was coming on a week's visit—the first time she had ever left the village. Cassie could not fail to look forward to the pleasures of showing her round, but she longed all the same for Gran. Gran was getting old, and what if she died and Cassie never saw her again?

The Garsides were going for a fortnight to the sea. That is, Mrs., with Miss Jean and the boy. Mr. Garside's play looked like running for ever, so they said, and he would look after himself during the week and catch a train on the two Sunday mornings, returning each Monday afternoon for the evening performance. Miss Jean had not managed to get another job, but it was a bad time of year, she said; things would look up in the autumn. Cassie thought the holiday a poor sort of adventure for her, no one of her own age to amuse her. Yet you could see as she made her preparations that she expected some shattering experience to overtake her while she was from home. Cassie could certainly not get her imagination round what the experience was expected to be. She sought, perhaps, if such a thing could be put into words, a means to encountering fame. She had sometimes seemed to speak of this, and did so again on the eve of the trip, when she was packing carefully with sheets and sheets of virgin tissue paper.

"By the time I come back I'll have an idea for a novel."

"Shall you really, miss?"

"I shall lie on the sand and become inspired."

Cassie smiled at her, feeling in some curious way a good deal older than this uncertain, struggling creature. It was as if she wanted to warn her.

"Will it be a love story or adventures?"

"Both."

Then she started piling up the books she intended taking with her, humping them along in a bag of their own, along with many notebooks and pads. She handed a rather tattered novel to Cassie.

"You can read this on your holiday, if you like."

Cassie looked at it doubtfully. The fact that it was old-looking suggested to her that it might be the sort of book they had been supposed to read at school.

"Is it the classics?" she asked.

"Lord, no! It's just a story. Only it's about the country, so you ought to enjoy it. If only I could write a book about the country!"

"Can't you?"

"No, I can't!"

"Did you ever try, then?"

"Yes. Oh yes—I've tried. I only know what I remember from when I was about twelve. I used to stay with old aunts. I know about smells and sounds, but I don't know how many of things. How many cows? How many hens? I don't even know how many men it takes to run a farm. You must know."

"It depend if it's a big farm."

"Well—a small farm."

"Yes. But how small?"

"Oh well—never mind."

"Thank you for loaning me the book," said Cassie, anxious to please her. She looked at the title, which made no sense. "What's it about?"

"About a girl with a harelip."

"Oh."

"Her father's a wizard."

"Goodness," said Cassie, more interested. "I know one o' them. Lives down riverwards."

"There you are, you see! Her father pretends he can raise up spirits and she has to help him. He says he can bring Venus into his own kitchen—so the girl has to be Venus. The man she loves is there."

"Oh, I see," lied Cassie.

"Well—I don't know really whether you'd like it. Don't feel you've got to read it. I don't really think as much of it as I did once. But I'm older than you. I loved it when I was your age."

"I'd be glad to read it, Miss Jean."

"Don't lose it. I still read bits of it sometimes."

"Oh I never would lose it." Cassie stood a moment more, holding the book awkwardly. "I hope you have a lovely time away."

"Thanks. It really depends on the weather," said Jean in an offhand way, as if she wished the recent conversation had never taken place.

"Why did I lend her *Precious Bane?* It was a silly thing to do. I never thought what it is really about until I started explaining the story. It's about the way men can't see anything until it is stripped and set before them."

Jean paused. She was scribbling late at night, everything but her journal packed and ready. She looked at what she had written and decided that its clarity and wisdom was the best thing she had ever achieved in all her writing life. It was as if a gold miner, already quite busy, had opened some glittering new seam. She would write more like that. More and more. Better and better. It would get better all the time.

60

At one o'clock she switched off her light and stretched herself in bed in a mood of delight, confidence and anticipation.

"I love the sea, the desolate sea. At seven I get up and go alone to bathe. This alarms Mother, who has only just been cured of standing on the tideline crying, 'Swim along and not out! Swim along and not out!' She'll be at it again once Roddy learns to swim. He can't at the moment and it sends him mad. . . . At five o'clock when the sun is slipping down the sky a bit, the serious swimmers come to the shore. The tide is full. They have been waiting for it all day. They waste no time. They strip off their beach gowns and anchor them among the stones, then, throwing back their shoulders they advance as though they had been walking on pebbles ever since they were born. They go in smoothly, they swim and swim, strong and indifferent. . . . The other evening there was one towel on the beach when all the rest had gone. I thought that swimmer had swum too far, would never return, and ought I to do something about it? I was on the beach alone, tasting the lovely salt and the dried sun on my lips mouth. I decided there was nothing I could do. Just as I left, a little old woman swam in calmly, wrapped herself up and went smooth and unhurried in the direction of the awful hotel. I followed her, though not to the awful hotel. After the stones, the feel and the silence as you step onto the paving. . . ."

At this point Jean broke off, for she could not find the image that she needed. She read through what she had written. Gloom swept her. Of all those words *dried sun* were the only two worth having; even the substitution of *mouth*, though so much stronger than *lips*, struck her as painfully purple. She knew she should tear off the sheet and toss it into the wastepaper basket. But it would have seemed like drowning a newborn kitten.

Cassie went with her father to meet Queenie at Liverpool Street station. She did not know at all why she felt less excited than frightened. Suppose she had not remembered right? Or suppose Queenie had changed so much in these months of parting that by now she could not be recognized?

Neither was the case. She stepped out of the train wearing a green print dress that had once been Margery's, and a round straw hat that Cassie herself had not seen fit to bring into a new life. Anyone could see she was Queenie.

"Well, Cass?" said Queenie, frightened in her turn.

"How's my girl?" asked their father; as he always did. How's my girl? How's my boy? How's my old lady? The last to Gran.

"How's Gran?" asked Cassie, walking beside Queenie down the platform.

"Sent her love."

"She well, is she?"

"She say she tire easy. She fare to me all right, and all of us."

"You never wrote if she have my card for her birthday."

"I knew I'd be seeing you, Cassie."

"Did she?"

"What?"

"Did she get it? Did she get my card?" said Cassie, her voice rising.

"Yes, yes—she get it that very right morning. . . . Don't you nag me, Cassie Martle. Fare to me you changed a bit, all these months."

"Maybe I've changed for the better!" *Fare to me,* thought Cassie; I don't speak that way so much now. . . .

They walked on in silence, Dad ahead carrying Queenie's old case with the strap around it and a dangling label. It was like the worst parts of old times, and both girls were thinking so, the one blinking rapidly, the other biting her lip and swallowing. Rage, grief, disappointment stalked down the platform with them.

"Come on, now, you two," Dad called back to them. "Got to get home some time. You can do your chattering later."

Cassie shot a sideways glance at Queenie, just to see if his complete unawareness might make her smile. But Queenie chose dignity and looked blank.

Fortunately there was the tube train to distract her. Gradually she allowed her amazement at so much that was new to overcome her temper. First she talked only to Dad, but then she began darting questions and exclamations of surprise at Cassie.

"Then why's it called the underground?" she cried, as their train emerged disconcertingly into the open air.

"It's the District," said her father.

"What's that mean?"

63

"We get off here," said Dad.

Later, when they were in the room they were to share, that Mum had made nice with a vase of flowers and everything spick and clean, they were sisters again—separated sisters with so much to ask and answer that they gabbled one another down and could hardly bear to stop for tea, though it was Mum's best.

Queenie had not met Mum before today. "Is she all right, then?"

"Nice. She's nice."

"Not like our own, though."

"You never knew our own. I'm two year older and I don't remember. She make a good home for our Dad. She've a kind heart, Queenie. I can't say fairer."

Queenie sat silent through tea, however, answering when she was spoken to, but briefly; eating slowly, as if everything she bit into was dry and would not be swallowed. Cassie remembered her as a small child, rolling the food round and round her mouth, refusing to swallow it, sitting at the table and Gran sitting with her until either she swallowed in despair or spat in defiance. A small remembering smile just touched Cassie's mouth. The way people went on!

That night they lay in bed talking and talking. The family news, the village news, tumbling from Queenie with such force it seemed almost to bounce between them.

Suddenly Dad thumped on the wall and shouted.

"It's long past midnight! Be quiet, now, can't you?"

They giggled and continued in whispers. Then slept.

Queenie's dearest wish next morning was to see where

Cassie worked. So they walked through the side streets that Cassie now knew so well, and came to Stanton Avenue.

"Here," said Cassie, pausing at No. 15.

"Oh—it's not big. I thought for sure it'd be a big house."

"There's no room for big houses just here," said Cassie, reasonably enough.

"I see." The disappointment in Queenie's voice and expression was very galling to Cassie.

"There's a lovely bathroom. You don't need to go all down the garden to the privy. Mrs. Garside make all those curtains herself on the sewing machine."

"It look very clean," Queenie conceded.

At this moment the door opened and out came Mr. Garside.

"Well—it's Edith. Good morning," he said in his big friendly voice. "Can't stay away from work, is that it?" His laugh boomed.

"It's my sister, sir. Queenie. I come to show her where I work so she can tell Gran."

"Come in, then! And how are you, Queenie? You're very like your sister, I see. . . . I'm just off up to town, Edith. Be sure to shut the door properly when you leave."

He nodded and smiled warmly and then was away up the road, tall, broad; looking different—but not nearly different enough for Queenie to spot that he was an actor. In fact she had really hardly taken in the fact that such outlandish persons existed. Film stars, yes; but that was quite different, you couldn't really call them people, just pictures of themselves.

"He forgot your name!" she burst out, as they went indoors.

"Edith's my name. Like yours is Joyce. Edith's a better name for living in London."

"But you're Cassie! You're not Edith, you're Cassie! You're Cassie!"

"Keep your hair on," said Cassie rudely. "Look—here's the parlor. They say sitting room. Nice, isn't it?"

"It's plain."

"That's right. They like it plain. So do I." She had begun to sound cross and defiant. She wished they had not come, or at least that Mr. Garside had not let them in. "Come into the kitchen, do. You won't see any more by looking longer."

Everything was tidy in the kitchen. Mr. Garside was not one to leave things lying about. There was not so much as one dirty knife to be seen. He was a very neat, tidy person and seemed to have few possessions. Sometimes there was a library book of his on the bedside table, but that was all. The kitchen looked bright and welcoming, the sun had come out after a gray start and was pouring indoors. On the windowsill was Cassie's knitting rolled up inside a paper bag.

"Left that behind. I'll take that with me."

"What're you knitting?"

"It's a pullover for young Roddy. That's a surprise for Christmas."

"You like him, do you?"

"He's a demon," said Cassie fondly.

Now she was easy again. The place became her own. She led Queenie from room to room, pointing out, explaining, proud. She was quite at home here now. Nothing they did struck her any longer as strange. The more she talked about them the better pleased she felt, not only with them but with herself. She had again that belonging feeling. First she had begun to feel they belonged to her, then that she belonged to them. But as she spoke of them to Queenie it was as if they all belonged together and whatever happened to any one of them, wherever she and they went afterward, something would be left that had come out of them as they were now. Like ghosts, was as far as she could have explained.

They looked into Mr. and Mrs. Garside's big room, and into the little boy's room that was tiny and stuffed full of toys and books and pictures on the wall. Then Cassie showed her own room, wishing it were bigger yet displaying it with satisfaction. Then there was the bathroom and the lavatory to be inspected. Only Miss Jean's door remained unopened, and Cassie did not particularly want Queenie to go in there. She had not felt they were intruding anywhere else, but she felt it here. She sidled past the closed door and started down the stairs. But Queenie, now very much at ease, opened the door without asking and went inside.

"Is this hers?" she called back to Cassie.

"Whose?"

"Jean, of course."

"Yes, that's Miss Jean's room. There's nothing much to look at, so come on down."

"It smell of cigarettes."

Cassie clicked her tongue and came back up the stairs.

"Doesn't have to ask your permission, does she? She

can smoke a cigarette in her own room if she want, can't she?"

"Turkish!" cried Queenie, cleverly recognizing an ultimate sophistication, if not a hint of vice.

"What do you know about Turkish cigarettes, Queenie Martle?"

"Lady Gwen smokes Turkish."

"Oh—so you're in with the Grange set, are you?"

"I took a parcel of washing. . . . It's a nice room, Cass," she decided. "I see what you said. They do like that plain, don't they? Still—nice. Fancy black paint!"

"She say it frame the gray walls."

"Bit like a funeral card, though."

In spite of herself, Cassie laughed.

"Come on down, Queenie. We can make a cup of tea if you like."

"More like a sitting room than a bedroom."

"Well, that's what it is. She sit here doing her writing."

"What—letters?"

"She write books, Queenie, so there. . . . Oh come on down, do. And shut the door, can't you?"

It was an hour more before they left the house. If they didn't take care, Cassie said, they'd be late for dinner.

"Does she get cross? Does Mum get cross, Cassie?"

"I never see her yet. Better not try and find out." Cassie closed the front door very carefully, and took hold of the letter box and shook it to see that the lock had worked properly. It was her house as she left it and walked down the narrow path to the gate. "We'll go by the shops. I'll buy us ices."

68

As she spoke, Cassie turned up toward the main road and then stopped short. Somebody she knew was walking toward her.

"Well—hullo! Hullo, Cassie. Fancy seeing you."

"Fancy!" She stepped slightly behind Queenie, as if to use her as some sort of shield. "This is Queenie. She's my sister. She's staying for the week. It's Len Eversley, Queenie."

Queenie did not reply, but merely stared in amazement and possibly admiration.

"I was just passing on my holiday," Len explained—if you could call it an explanation—for Stanton Avenue seemed a curious spot to spend a holiday. "I remember now—you work here, don't you?"

His falseness made her smile, though not openly. He seemed taller than ever and both his eyes showed today, since his hair had disappeared under a cap. He looked mild, anxious.

"It's everybody's holiday," Cassie said. "It's Queenie's holiday and it's mine and it's Garside's holiday and my friend Elsie's holiday. Well—it's August and that's why."

"I've got a week," he said.

"I've got two. Queenie's got a week." She smiled and spoke out of Miss Jean's mouth—"Well, I must fly." But she dallied. "We're getting the bus at the top. Len's going to be a bus conductor, Queenie."

Queenie opened her mouth—then closed it in defeat. Len went with them to the stop, talking about buses fondly but without much continuity, as if filling in until he said what he really wanted to say.

"Having a good time, are you?" Cassie asked him.
"What do you do with yourself all day? I bet you get
under your mum's feet all right."

It seemed more likely that his mum would be under his
feet, but the silly remark worked its magic.

"Out a lot. Kew Gardens. You ever go to Kew Gardens?
Cassie—did you ever walk along the river to Kew
Gardens?"

"No, I never did. Not yet. Nice, is it?"

"Very nice. It's very nice. Tell you what," he burst out,
as if it had just occurred to him, "we could Saturday.
You be here at the bus stop Saturday after dinner."

"I might."

There was a bus bearing down on them now—she
would not have risked offending him by waiting for a
pirate today.

"Come on, Queenie! We don't want to miss it. All
right, Len. Two-thirty Saturday."

She waved to Len from the step of the bus, hanging
back like Persephone as she was borne away.

Sitting at dinner, where the steak-and-kidney pudding
ran rivers of glorious gravy, the suet crust melted on the
tongue, the meat was, as Gran would say, tender as an
Earl's baby, Queenie spoke of Len.

"Who's Len, dear?" Mum asked Cassie.

"He come to that church dance I went with Elsie."

"Nice, is he?"

"He's all right, I daresay."

"Guess what," said Queenie. "He's a bus conductor."

"How old, then?" asked Dad.

"Old enough to be a bus conductor," Cassie cried.

"He'll need to be over twenty-four," said Dad.

"All right, then—he's twenty-four and a bit, I suppose. Anyway—he's only learning. I told you, Queenie—he's *going* to be a bus conductor, I said."

"Going to Kew Gardens with him Saturday," Queenie said.

"Kew! Oh that's very nice, dear. I say Kew's ever such a lovely place, isn't it, Dad? Saturday? Good thing Queenie's not off home till the Monday."

Both sisters opened their mouths. Queenie looked quickly at Cassie, but Cassie gave her no help. Cassie had a dreamy feeling, as though matters had best be left to go their own way. She sat back and waited, not only unable to make any effort, but far from certain what that effort ought to be.

"Did he mean me, too, Cass?" Queenie labored.

Mum laughed. "Of course he must've. If he's any manners, that is. Seeing you were there at the time of asking."

"I expect so," Cassie said.

She still sat there, just smiling, now; remembering that he had gone to Stanton Avenue in search of her, remembering his uncertain manner. A bus conductor, indeed! He'd never learn to shout out loud enough, he just wasn't that bellowing sort of chap. She sat wondering what else he could do, thinking about him in an easy idle way, and contemplating the visit to Kew Gardens. She barely noticed the decked-out trifle that had taken the place of the steak-and-kidney pudding. She did not speak again until the meal was over and Dad had gone back through the door out of the kitchen to open up the shop for the afternoon's business.

Then Queenie pulled her aside, saying anxiously, "Is that all right? Kew Gardens? Is that all right?"

"Why not?"

5

"WE SHOULD really ought to have come first thing," Len said.

They went in through the turnstile and gave up one penny apiece. Len paid. Within the great encircling walls they could hardly hope to be the only ones. Especially on a Saturday afternoon in August.

"There's no one, really, at opening time," Len explained. "Very quiet. I like it then. I like it now—but I like it then."

"Well, if you'd rather be on your own I'm sure Queenie and me can walk the other way round!"

He grinned, though faintly. "Asked you to come, didn't I?"

There was the least emphasis on *you*. He had looked more than merely surprised when he saw that Queenie was with Cassie; but he had quickly rearranged his features into a smile of greeting. No doubt of it, he was a nice boy, decent and kind. As it turned out, Queenie had barely to be reckoned with, since she remained mute as a swan from the time of setting out to the time of turning for home. Cassie and Len walked and talked together and Queenie walked a pace or two behind—not sulking, just silent. Every now and again Cassie looked back, crying, "Come *on*, Queenie."

At this moment of the declining summer the gardens were past their best. Yet they held most magically enshrined the devotion and the skill, the hopes and the fears of all those unknowns whose life consisted solely in making things grow in beauty. The accumulation of carefully collected and nurtured plants and shrubs and trees made of themselves a pattern and a purpose full of color and design so gentle and so subtle that none of these three visitors observed it. Len kept saying, "You should see it in spring—lilac, rhododendrons, daffodils, all those things." He knew a lot of names that the country-bred sisters had never even heard. Cassie listened to him in respectful amazement, while Queenie hung behind, forever inspecting trees with curious barks, running her fingers up and down the strange textures, feeling them tenderly with her fingertips like a blind girl reading Braille. By wide waters geese ran, not the robust and angry geese familiar to Cassie and Queenie, but geese of strange color and marking. Only their habit was the same, the neck undulating, the open beak and hissing, disapproving cry, the honk of annoyance that any should stand there staring, pointing, laughing—and offering no crust in tribute. They were aristocrats. They had never learned of village greens and small muddy ponds.

"A bit like home, is it?" Len asked.

"No!" Cassie shook her head violently and laughed, calling back to her sister, "Len ask if it remind us of home!"

Queenie gave a shrill laugh in her turn, her one contribution to the day, and the geese turned away instantly and moved off fast.

"I like the country," Len said. "Sometimes I know for sure I'd like to live in the country."

"You never would. There's nothing to do. You'd never be a bus conductor. Well—you might. Only there's not so many buses."

Cassie had noticed with surprise how many people spoke of living in the country as if it were some wonderful dream. It's quite like the country, it's almost in the country, Cassie had heard Elsie say, describing some spot where her newly married cousin hoped to live. It's nice for the children, they said; nothing like a country up-bringing. . . . And all the time another seven rows or so of little houses pushed out to cover the fields and rob them of their green forever.

"How's your friend Elsie?" Len asked. "Is she away on her holiday, then? Where'd she go?"

"She had a week home, then her people took her to look after the children. That's Bognor, where they are."

They were sitting on green-painted iron chairs at an iron table covered with a white cloth. The cloth was clipped to the edge of the table so that it would not blow away, and it flapped and fluttered, but in a well-ordered way. There were many tables, nearly all occupied. The chairs scraped horribly on the gravel as people sat down and tugged them into position, or shoved them back, even more roughly and noisily, as they rose to leave. Trees supplied a gentle dappling shade, there was a pleasant bustle and murmur, with quiet laughter, the clatter of thick cups on thick saucers, the chink of teaspoons.

Sometimes a snatching child was rebuked, there was a slap and a screech. If the desired bun fell to the ground during the encounter, then a hundred little birds swooped instantly and began squabbling and screeching in their turn. At a conversational level voices were curiously muffled, losing themselves among the heavy-leaved branches or spreading softly across the surrounding lawns.

"I like it here, Len."

"I thought you'd be reminded of home, though."

"Oh no—I like it because it's something else. Mum was right—she say this was a nice place to go."

Len smiled. He pressed both girls to cakes and chocolate biscuits. Cassie could see that he was liking it, too, even though Queenie sat there like a stuffed rabbit.

"One Saturday we could come early," he said, harking back.

Then they realized that the holidays would soon be over and Saturdays would be working days.

"There's places to go Sundays, Cassie. Box Hill. We can take a bus to Box Hill."

"What for? For the boxing?"

"Don't make me laugh!" Len said.

Cassie reclined in the hard little chair, the back of it bit into her shoulders, it could hardly have been more uncomfortable, almost painful—but warm content possessed her. She lazily held out her hand with crumbs spread on the palm and a dozen sparrows and finches came to fight over the dainties. The feel of their pin-frail feet delighted her, and the brisk rush of their wings as they came and went. She picked up her crumby plate and tipped what was left on to the ground. Down came the flock to peck and squabble.

Only suddenly, out of kindly sunshine, a large bird swooped, and seized a sparrow as if it, too, were a crumb, and carried it up shrieking into the branches.

Len looked stricken. "What was that?"

"That was a jay."

The jay sat concealed among the leaves and tore apart its prey, and through the warm air a few feathers, a fragment or two of down, lightly floated to the ground and were blown about at random.

Cassie had never been to the seaside. She wondered about it, wondered about the Garsides there—were they enjoying themselves, was the weather as good as it was here, had Miss Jean thought of a story to write . . . ? At the seaside, everything must be different. So it was different; but in a way it was the same.

"Very surprising. Extraordinary. We looked out for D. this morning (she could no longer bring herself to call him Daddy but thought Father stuffy), and instead of coming swinging along from the station he arrived by car. Who was driving him? Well, it was Anthony Lincoln, one of that family that moved into the corner house in Grantham Gardens. Mother knows Mrs. slightly—no doubt, she *decided* to know her because she has two un-married sons! This one of them has just bought a car—would that we had so!—and having got into conversation with D. because he goes a lot to the theater and had recognized him, said he wanted to take his new car for a spin and would he go, too. So they spun in this direction. He'd brought his swimming things, so there were five of us on the beach in the afternoon. I wore my pale blue bathing suit. It makes me look very brown.

"Anthony Lincoln is about twenty-five. No one could call him handsome. He has a slightly crooked nose—broken in a rugger scrum, he says, but I daresay most men with broken noses say that—and he sneezes a lot because of it. Wanted to be an architect, turned out to be a chartered accountant.

"In the afternoon a thing happened that never happened to me before. There was a bit of a swell on, it was fine but there was a breeze off the shore, and the tide was turning and I suddenly found myself getting into difficulties, as the papers say. The water seemed immensely deep and the tide furiously strong and I was sure I should drown. I don't suppose I should have done really, but it's nice to think that Anthony saved my life by grabbing hold of me and pushing me to shore. Well, perhaps he did?

"He was very decent about it, and said nothing, just pretended it hadn't really happened. No one had noticed anything because they were busy getting into conversation with some other parents with a boy about Roddy's age. M., who is a rather shy person really, will always go into battle to find R. friends. In a way I suppose she was doing the same for me when she contrived to meet Mrs. Lincoln.

" 'We'll go and get a drink, shall we?' A.L. said.

"We just walked off, smiling at the parents, who doubtless thought we were off for a nice sharp walk. Instead, A. took me to the awful hotel. It seemed less awful than expected—wonder why?!—and I found all that red plush rather comforting. We were early and the bar was not open, so we sat around until the time came. I was determined not to be silent so I often sounded quite idiotic. In due course A. ordered martinis and I swallowed the cherry whole somehow or other and it stuck a bit. I had to make a superhuman effort and pray as well, and I got it down without actually choking. My nose ran, then, and just for a second I thought I had come out without a hanky.

"A. said something about being an actress.

" 'No, I'm an author, really.' I said, 'I'll never be an actress. Not a good one, anyway.'

" 'Oh I don't know,' he said. 'You did quite a good drowning scene.'

"Just for a moment I thought he meant I'd put it on for his benefit. I nearly died. But then I decided he was letting me off being a bad swimmer into the bargain.

"So then he asked me, since I was an author (!) what I like reading. What did I think of Gilbert Frankau?

"I didn't know *what to* say, except that I'd never read anything of his, which was true, but it seemed so awful, when he said, What was I reading at the moment? to say *Anna Karenina* that I said, *The Constant Nymph*. Well, I do love it.

" 'I loved the play,' he said. 'I thought Edna Best was marvelous. She looked so young. That gym dress! And all the death scene. . . . Oh dear.'

"When I stayed the night with Philippa H. after the

ghastly Carter party she told me men are much more sentimental than women and cry terribly easily at unreal things.

" 'Did it make you cry?' I asked A.

" 'Well, there was some sort of fluid in and around the old eyes,' he said.

"He has a rather nice way of shutting his eyes till they are slits and laughing silently. You can see the amusement in the slit and it is really rather attractive.

" 'Did you see *The Nymph* early in the run?' I asked next, thinking the remark sounded professional—I only realized about this professional language business the other day; I suppose as I've grown up with it I don't notice it. But quite ordinary things like *front of the house* or *ring down* seem to make people frown in a respectful way as they try to work it out.

" 'About a month ago,' he said.

" 'So Coward was out of it.'

"He said he'd seen the new chap. 'Not bad,' he said. 'Really not at all bad.'

"As I and a great many others *know* that the new chap is going to be a great actor, I sneered a bit at this.

" 'He's marvelous,' I said coldly.

" 'Well, the chap was no gent, was he—Lewis Dodd, I mean—letting that poor girl open the window when she had a bad heart.'

"So we sat there absolutely racked with laughter after that, and he fetched two more martinis, and this time I was careful with the cherry. I had to be a bit careful about everything, actually, and felt somewhat tottery as we walked back to join the family.

"We had a horrible small-hotel Sunday supper. Then Anthony drove off waving, leaving his passenger behind to catch a train tomorrow morning. . . .

"I have been thinking about Cassie and her bus conductor."

Queenie went home on the Monday. Cassie went to the station to see her off. Dad was busy with the shop and had said Mum should go with the girls. But Mum was wiser and left them to go off on their own.

"Won't you ever come back?" Queenie asked Cassie, when her seat was chosen, her bag stowed, and they were standing wretchedly on the platform not looking at one another.

"How do I know?"

"Fare to me you like your old Garsides better than us."

"That's different."

"You'll never marry a London boy—you'll never live in London for ever?"

"What if I did?"

"Oh Cassie. . . ."

"Don't say that to Gran, though."

"He say he'd like to live in the country."

"Who say?"

"Len, of course."

"I only met him two or three times, Queenie."

"Then it's still Ned, is it? Is it?"

Cassie was quiet for a moment. "*What*'s still Ned? What are you on about, Queenie Martle?"

"He said to send his love. . . ."

"Ned did? You take a long time to remember that."

"Well—I remember that now."

"He shouldn't talk so soft. Me and Ned never had any understanding."

"Oh Cassie!" cried Queenie, falling on her neck and beginning to cry. "Come home! Come home!"

Cassie could not answer. The thought of home was like the promise of a hot bath to aching limbs. And Gran —and Gran. . . . Eighty since her birthday a few weeks ago. Eighty was old. The holiday was over and there could not be a visit till this time next year. A year seemed very long. Perhaps she could work all week and buy nothing new and save up her money and her days off so that she could go sooner?

"They'd let me come if Gran was ill," she said. "Don't you forget that. Any time she seem bad you must tell me. I'll come even if I lose my job. Only I never would— they're not like that. . . . Did you write down the phone number like I tell you?"

"Yes, Cassie. Yes, I did."

"Don't lose it, then. Better give it Jack, Queenie. Blow your nose. You must get in. They're shutting the doors."

A shouting porter came along the length of the train, slamming the doors and testing each handle. Queenie stood in the window of the compartment with the tears now running freely, her whole face shone with grief and misery. Despair touched Cassie. If she might only drag open the door and scramble aboard, and feel the train move off, strong as ten thousand great horses, snorting with confidence, pulling out of the station on the long journey home. . . .

"Don't, dear," she said to Queenie.

"Shall I give him your love, then? Shall I give Ned your love, Cassie. His mother took ever so sick last month."

"You could have said! What happen?"

"Took her to hospital. But she come back safe."

"Then tell him—tell Ned I felt sorry to hear of it."

The train began to move and the sisters to wave, at first slowly and miserably, then frantically as distance increased between them.

When—when. . . . Oh when again. . . ?

Mum looked up as Cassie came indoors.

"That young man of yours came calling."

"What young man of mine?"

"Oh—well, now. Got so many, have we? Len, I mean. It's Len, isn't it? Very nice mannered. He went into the shop and bought cigarettes! Laugh! I said to Dad—you can see through that one like a pane of glass." She laughed warmly. "I say, you can see through that one!"

"Oh, Mum—anyone'd think . . . I only met him about twice."

"Well you'll meet him again for sure. I asked him to tea Sunday."

"Oh, *Mum*! You shouldn't've."

"There now," said Mum, bristling a little, "there's some that's hard to please. I thought you'd like it if he got asked."

"Mind your own silly business!" shouted Cassie, looking with loathing at poor Mum, turning on her heel, flinging out of the room, slamming the door hard behind her so that the whole house shook—just as if she were Miss Jean Garside—tearing up the stairs and into the room Mum had said should always be called Cassie's room.

She threw herself on the bed she had shared with Queenie and seemed to smell her still on the pillow and where the sheet turned back. It was the smell of home, of smoke from the kitchen fire that always burned, of honey, of warm sweat from running fast and laughing down the village street, earth from pulled lettuce, the special scent of beans. . . .

Cassie cried out aloud, wailing, "I want to go home! I want to go home! Oh please God, let me go home! Oh Gran! Oh Gran, Gran, Gran!"

"There now," said Mum, who had come up after her, who was not put off, who sat on the bed and pulled Cassie into her arms and rocked her and smoothed her hair. "There now—there now . . . Oh Cassie—Cassie, dearie, quiet! Quiet! You'll upset your dad. He'll hear right down the shop. . . ."

"When can I go home?" cried Cassie, not struggling now, but sobbing and weeping soaking tears all over poor Mum.

"There now, there," was all Mum could find to say.

Cassie leaned against her and thought how Queenie would soon be there, the train stopping, the small silent station. Out she would get, carrying her strapped case, and in the yard there would be someone waiting to drive her home. It could be Jack, in his old gray van that he used for work. It could even be Ned Gooderham, with the squat little cart his grandfather had built, and old dapple Dumpy still between the shafts, though she was going on twenty-three. . . .

Cassie stopped crying, pulled back from Mum and scrubbed at her eyes.

"Sorry."

"I thought you'd settled, dear. So did Dad. We thought you'd got quite happy, working for Mrs. Garside."

"I am. I have."

"Oh Cassie, you couldn't leave them, dear. That nice Mrs. Garside and the little boy—and you quite like Miss Jean, don't you, now?"

"I'm all right, Mum. I'm better."

"There isn't anything . . . ? Mr. Garside. . . . You don't have any sort of difficulty—?"

"*No I don't!* I know what you think—about he's an actor and that. He's more a gentleman than any I might name."

"Well, then," said Mum, helpless and unhappy, wishing, perhaps, that Cassie were her own—she, for one reason and another, having left such matters much too late. "Well, then, Cass dear. . . ."

The day the Garsides were due home, Cassie went back to Stanton Avenue in the morning, Dad carrying her bag, and let herself in to No. 15 with the key she had collected earlier from Mr. Garside.

"They'll be back tea time, Dad."

"You'll be doing the shopping, then."

"Yes. I'll go now," said Cassie. Something strange in the words hung on her ear. She seemed to hear Queenie's voice, busy with the old usage. "I'll now go," she corrected herself. "Good-bye, Dad. And thanks for everything."

"Be good," he said. "Take care of yourself. God bless you, Cass." He went down the path to the gate and turned there, smiling rather sheepishly, saying softly, "That's a nice boy, that Len. You could do a lot worse, my girl."

Cassie did not answer. She smiled and waved.

At four-thirty or so, just as planned, Mrs. Garside, Miss Jean and Master Roddy drew up at the gate in a car hired to bring them from Victoria Station.

Cassie opened the door. She was smiling. Her pleasure in seeing them again could not be measured. The little boy rushed at her and she flung her arms round him. Mrs. Garside was smiling as she advanced up the path. She looked very well, there was that prettiness about her that was the far echo of her youth. Miss Jean looked topping. She was splendidly sunburned and her hair was bleached by sun and sea to a dazzling blond. She looked wonderful. She looked quite different. Cassie saw at once that something had happened to Miss Jean that had changed her life.

6

IN SEPTEMBER Cassie began going out regularly with Len. They went on Wednesday evenings to the cinema, the fine weather being now almost past. By October they were meeting more often, for he came to Dad's place for Sunday dinner when it was Cassie's Sunday off, and in the afternoon they went for a walk. In October, too, though she had had very little news from home, Cassie received a picture postcard from Ned Gooderham.

"Dear Cassie, This is to tell you poor Mother died a week Saturday. I hope you are well. Ned."

She sent a postcard in reply, with a picture of Westminster Abbey; it seemed more suitable than his posy of poppies and corn, which brought more of a reminder of home than a message of grief.

"Dear Ned, I am sorry to hear that. I hope the end come peaceful. You will be sad. From Cassie."

What would he do now? Live all alone in the cottage which would surely be his; or pack up and go away, as many did in search of better work than his at Clare's Farm. Or live, not alone, but with a wife. She thought over the girls who might be eligible, but her mind, unwilling, changed the subject.

For the Garsides, too, there were changes as the autumn went on. Miles Garside's play finished and he was at home with nothing to do. He went every day to his club, however, which was a club for actors—so that people would know he was still alive and in the market—so Miss Jean said. She was in a cheerful mood as she had had a stroke of good fortune just as her father's was running out.

"Shakespeare *again*," Cassie told Elsie.

"What's it called!"

"Much To Do About Nothing."

"That doesn't make a lot of sense."

"It sound all right when she tell me." It had also sounded subtly different, but though Cassie frowned and pondered she could not recall how.

"Just standing about again, is she, Cass?"

"No. She has to say something. She's a girl called Ursula."

"Better go and see her, then." Elsie gave a huffing, disapproving sigh. "Why can't she get herself into something funny?"

Cassie's day changed with the autumn. Young Roddy went to a different school—a proper school, Cassie would have said, all boys. There was an end to afternoon walks. It was about time, Cassie thought; but she knew she would miss seeing Elsie, even though she was in a gloomy mood just now, for dancing Alan had vanished from her life. Cassie felt quite guilty about Len because of Elsie, she thought it very hard for a girl to introduce a friend to a boy, and to see them going steady—and then to lose her own.

Sometimes, by an arrangement entered into between

Mrs. Garside and Mrs. Richardson, Elsie came and spent
the evening with Cassie, or Cassie went to the Richardsons' house. They sat together and knitted furiously and
Elsie went on discussing life, as she had done when they
met during the summer on the common. With Mr. Garside home in the evenings Cassie had more to do, but
Elsie was always ready to help her with the washing-
up. What was nicer was when the Garsides went out for
the evening; the two girls could then use the sitting room
and listen to the wireless. They both enjoyed the variety
programs and it was useful to have something to make
Elsie laugh. They liked Flotsam and Jetsam, and Tommy
Handley; and the man who said, "Can you hear me,
moother?" when he began his act. And the dance bands.
Elsie liked the Savoy Orpheans, but Henry Hall was
more in Cassie's line. The Garsides had to be out late for
the two girls to share a dance band—for Elsie always
stayed till they returned, when Mr. Garside never let
her walk home alone but saw her safely to the corner of
Knaresborough Road, where the Richardsons lived at No.
24.

"Where is it this time?" Elsie always asked eagerly
when she arrived and found Cassie alone.

It was disappointing when Cassie answered that they
had gone to the Lincolns since it meant they would not
be very late home. That was a disappointment to Elsie,
not only because of the dance music, but because she felt
grand being escorted through the innocent small streets
by a man who had his name in the papers. Still, there
was always some interest in a visit by the Garsides to the
Lincolns.

"How's she getting on? How's it going?"

"How should I know?"

"Oh go on, Cassie—d'you think he's serious? I can't understand it if he is. A great tall girl like her."

"What's wrong? He's taller."

"Just."

"That fare to me enough," said Cassie, sharply. She corrected herself, "That seems to me tall enough."

"What's he like? Last time he came here you said you didn't like him much."

"Makes eyes a bit," Cassie admitted. "But he always sit next to her, and that. It's his mother I'd worry about. She's a madam if ever I saw. Very friendly and all, but she likes to make Miss Jean look small."

"Pity she don't," said Elsie giving a whooping laugh.

Cassie did not respond.

When Cassie went out with Len to the pictures she always wore something smart. She dreaded appearing to him as a dowdy girl from the country, though he was certainly no gents'-outfitter's dream and his sister, with whom he lodged, and whom Cassie had met just once, might never have heard of fashion. Cassie's wardrobe was growing most miraculously. She spent her all on clothes. She knew Mrs. Garside disapproved. "Another new dress, Edith?" But Miss Jean egged her on. "You need a brown jumper to wear with that skirt. Match your eyes."

Cassie might say, "Oh go on, Miss Jean," but she was pleased and flattered.

Cassie talked to Len about Miss Jean.

90

"You'd never think she could have such a temper," she told Len. "The things she say!"

"What sort of things?"

She said cruel, wounding, bitter things, as wounding to herself as to any opponent, but Cassie found it hard to explain exactly.

"Dreadful things. I don't know."

"What's he say back at her?"

This, too, Cassie found hard to answer. Though Jean's father would at such time sound furious, it was a little as if he was acting an angry father and could stop and be himself at any moment he chose. Cassie had begun to feel that the rages of both should not be taken too seriously, and she was convinced that they could very often break off and burst out laughing if they chose. It was as though their quarrels were scenes written for them that had to be played to the final line. . . . Not that Cassie had worked that bit out, not yet, anyway.

It was nice that Len took an interest. Each time they met he asked how everyone was—Dad, Mum, the Garsides, Elsie.

"Does she miss Alan?" he asked one evening.

"Why should she? There's plenty more where that one come from."

"I saw him Thursday."

"Oh yes?"

"Got a good job. Hammond's Garage. Putney. Mechanic."

"That's nice."

Len was silent and thoughtful. They were nearing the

cinema and there was a bit of queue for the evening performance. Cassie always liked to see a queue—if there was none she would decide in advance that the film was a dud. The cinema was newly built and had colored lights that kept changing while the Wurlitzer organ played.

"Alan's got a motor bike," said Len, as they joined the queue.

It was the first time Cassie had heard him sound anything but easy and content. His longing for just such a wonderful toy seemed to come right out of him in a silent groan, a groan of envy.

"Never mind," she said. "You'll have a whole bus."

It was quite the wrong thing to have said.

"I should've tried for a driver, Cass. It's the driver's the important one."

To distract him, she asked if Alan had a new girl as well as a new job.

"Can't afford one, he says."

By now the queue was on the move and they shifted inside. The manager, wearing a dinner jacket, was supervising his more expensive patrons, calling many of them by name, turning adroitly from one to the next, with something like a click of his patent-leather heels. Soon Cassie and Len were into the darkness and shuffling blindly along the row into their seats.

"Cheer up," said Cassie, not liking his mood.

She put her hand on his arm and he took the hand and held it, turning to smile at her quickly, the light from the screen somehow increasing the gentleness of his expresson. Thus hand in hand they sat through the *Movietone News*, which was divided between the King and Queen bowing from a carriage, marching Germans and autumn fashions. Everyone laughed at the autumn fashions, but not as much as they had laughed at the soldiers. The man in the seat behind now leaned forward and politely asked Cassie if she would remove her hat. That meant she had also to remove her hand from Len's. Just as well, perhaps. They had never held hands before and enough was enough. She would not like him to think her forward. Her mind slid to Jean Garside. She and Mr. Lincoln had been to the pictures together at least once. Cassie could not decide whether Miss Jean would be stand-offish or too eager; but she felt sadly sure she would not manage things very well.

Then the news was done with and Mickey Mouse filled the screen, the sharp black and white of the cartoon quite dazzling after the fuzzy news pictures. After that it was the B picture, which this week was a Western. Len got quite worked up, as young Roddy Garside would, but Cassie worried about the overridden horses. She was glad when it was the big picture, Ramon Novarro falling in love in some sunny clime, all orange trees and sand. There were some lovely dresses, even there in the desert. Cassie hoped Elsie would see the picture, so that they could discuss which were the best bits. Elsie's home being in the neighborhood, she and her sisters went out together if their various free times coincided.

When they came out of the cinema the cold October sky was dazzling bright with stars and the air seemed like clean flowing water. Len's sister and her husband lived some way away, in a street near the railway line, but he walked home first with Cassie. Usually he paused on the corner and they stood a few moments, fishing up a remark or two to delay their parting. Then she went off toward No. 15 and he stayed until she reached the gate, where she turned and waved, then went inside.

But tonight when she paused he went on, stopping only when they reached the gate. She wondered if he was going to kiss her and hoped not—because of the street lamp and because someone might look out of a window; and because a first kiss, by her rules, was a serious matter. However, he only took her hand and squeezed it hard, giving her an intense look which did not suit him at all and made her want to giggle.

"Well," he said, "here's to the next time."

"And a merry meeting!" cried Cassie, as expected.

She went quickly through the side gate and for some reason was glad when she got inside the kitchen.

There was a letter from home. It was from Marge—her writing was the same as Queenie's, only older. Marge had not written before. Gran? Cassie fumbled the letter open, afraid to read what was inside. Margery wrote that their brother Jack had got the sack. He was second stockman at Wishart's; a big farm but they were cutting down.

"It come just when him and Sally thought to be engaged," Marge wrote, "so poor them."

Now what would he do? There were only so many farms in any one place. Miss Jean had wanted to know how many men were needed to run a farm. The answer seemed fewer and fewer. Oh poor Jack! There'd be little casual work now, with the beet and potatoes all but lifted and much ground turned already. What if he had to go on the dole? Gran'd die of shame if he did, but there wouldn't be much keep for him at home, for there never had been. . . . Cassie was well accustomed to the brutalities of life at the level along which she had grown up—but once the older among them had started earning it had eased a bit. The grim fact remained that she herself had come to London because there were few jobs at home —at the Grange they had once employed ten servants, counting the outside men, and now they made do with four—lucky Marge to be one of them. It was the same at the Manor—and where did money go to, then, that rich people suddenly had less?

She returned to the letter which, in her distress at the news about Jack, she had all this time been holding unfinished.

"Gran say we must all help out, Cass, she ask me to ask if you could send a little—could you manage a few shillings, dear? Never worry if it has to be no you have your uniform and things given but that is expensive to live in London. Five shillings would be better than nothing every little helps."

Cassie felt a sorry chill. She had grown accustomed to having her own money to spend and there was never a week she went out but she saw something she would like to have for herself. And now the season had changed she needed warmer things. And it was worse than that. Christmas was ahead. She and Elsie had made elaborate plans about present-giving. Elsie had already bought a mouth-organ for Bruce and was knitting a jacket for the little girl. Cassie had finished Roddy's pullover. She had seen some scent done up in a bottle shaped like a cat that she meant to buy for Miss Jean. "It look like her Pusskin," she had said to Elsie.

There was only one bad thing in all this planning. When Cassie told Mum about it all she had flown off the handle.

"Well, I *don't* know! It's for Mrs. Garside to give you a present—*if she pleases*—not for you to give her one! I never heard such cheek!"

It was the first time Cassie had heard Mum sound the least bit cross and she felt very hardly done by. She had shut her mouth tight, wishing she had Miss Jean's quick flow of anger and knew how to bang about as she did. Cassie could only sulk and find no way of ridding herself of her anger. She took it back to No. 15 with her and now as she read Marge's request she felt it thumping about inside her. She felt very far from the girl she had been at home, she felt very far from home itself, where each of them had taken for granted that it was necessary to help the rest.

Reluctantly, Cassie looked in her purse. She had six shillings still, which was unusual by a Wednesday. In the little black tin cashbox, with its red and gold stripes and tiny key, where she kept her savings for the brief time they stayed with her, she had a pound note and some coppers. Elsie had taken her to a shop where you could buy clothes and pay a bit each week, and Cassie had already put down thirty shillings toward a coat and skirt. Unless she kept up the payments she would lose the thirty shillings *and* the coat and skirt. Also she needed warm gloves—she had lost the left hand of her last year's

pair—new ones would cost at least 3/11. The request
from home was a terrible threat to Cassie's riches, which
were her consolation for other things lost. This sad and
sinful selfishness upset her in its turn. She slept badly.
She rose with the feeling that she was a wretch unwilling
to help her own brother. She went about her work on the
brink of tears, burned the toast, let the milk boil over,
frizzled the bacon.

"What's the matter with Edith?" she heard Mr. Garside
ask; and Mrs. Garside answered, "She had a letter from
home by the last post. I hope there's nothing wrong."

Cassie was alarmed by this exchange. Suppose Madam
actually asked her if anything was wrong? To say that
her brother was out of work seemed in some way to put
him in an unfavorable light. People who lived in easier
circumstances could be very funny about the dole—they
comforted themselves that the unemployed were provided for but despised them for accepting what was
offered. Cassie had grown up knowing this. To say of a
man, "He's on the dole," was as much as to call him an
idle good-for-nothing.

While Cassie was cleaning away the breakfast and
struggling with her worries, Miss Jean came into the
kitchen. She brought a pair of shoes to clean. Cassie knew
this was only an excuse, as she was going to rehearsal and
would certainly not be wearing a pair of brown walking
shoes. There were times when Cassie felt far older and
wiser than Miss Jean, when she winced at her clumsiness
and would have liked to shield her from her follies. And
though this was only a faint and inarticulate murmur in
Cassie's mind, Jean, too, must have known there was a

feeling between them not ready to be defined, and that it was a candidate for the name of friendship.

Jean chattered a bit as she polished her shoes. She was not very good at the job, but then in Cassie's opinion only men knew how to clean shoes properly. At last she had either to say what she had come to say or go away. She put away the shoe-cleaning things in their box, very carefully and slowly, with a most uncharacteristic neatness. She had reached the door before desperation found words for her.

"Are you all right, Cassie?" was the best she could manage.

"Yes, thank you."

"I thought perhaps you'd got a headache."

"No, miss." Now Cassie was the one without the right words.

"Well—have you got a pain? I could let you have a couple of my pills."

This woman-to-woman approach melted Cassie.

"'Tisn't that. My sister write our brother Jack just lost his job."

"Oh *dear*! Oh that's awful for him! Everybody should be able to work—everybody! There should be jobs for everyone!" Jean cried, in the kind of voice Cassie had often heard on the wireless, a voice that was about politics.

"I don't know where Jack's to get his, I'm sure. That's not easy, not round about ours." She heard her own country voice forgetting its improvements, strangely contrasting with Miss Jean's strong tones and emphatic manner. "That's no fun for a great man—hanging about.

. . . Gran'll never put up with him on the dole, that's sure."

"But that's what it's there for, Cassie!"

"That's not the way Gran believe. My sister Marge say we must all help. So," said Cassie, seizing the chance to hear herself sound a brave and good sister, and so perhaps force herself to it, "I'll send a bit for Marge."

Jean said, speaking fast, "You'll need a postal order. There's one upstairs I've had for ages—never cashed it. You can have that."

"On no, Miss Jean. . . . How much is it?"

"Ten shillings. I'm sure you can't afford more."

Cassie bit her lip, her eyes stung. She had hesitated over five shillings and now she must send ten.

"It's a loan," Jean said. "I shan't want it back for ages. I can't *need* it, can I, if I haven't bothered to cash it?" She rushed on as if she dreaded what Cassie might say next, as if she knew all about pride, that could accept anything with a smile—except stupid money. "We get paid for rehearsals. I'm not penniless." She was almost scowling as she cried fiercely, "Please, Cassie! *Please!* *Please*, Cassie!"

Cassie very slowly smiled, very slightly, the merest hesitant movement of the corners of her mouth.

"If you like," she said.

"A good thing it happened yesterday and not today. Today we all turned up to rehearse in that awful dingy room in Cranborne Street and there was no one there, the place was locked. We all hung about outside, even Elizabeth Harman, though she was pretty haughty about it until she forgot her vanity and grew plain fed up and started swearing in a dainty way. Could hardly believe my ears, she looks so sweet and fragile, and really it worked up to quite a crescendo. At last Tommy Brent turned up—he's the management, I suppose, in a sort of a way. He said he was sorry but the backers had backed out. There were a few pounds in the kitty, he said. So we all went into the nearest ABC and had coffee and he doled out what there was. Elizabeth did not come, she swept off in a taxi, crying, 'You know where you can always find me, darling,' and someone said, 'In bed.' Honestly. . . . My share of the money was a pound, but Mary and Ronnie and Gerald, who were only dancing and walking on, only got ten shillings.

"So now I'm unemployed, like Cassie's brother Jack.

"When I got home and told M. about it I said I thought I'd go on the dole, and she turned pale and told me to behave myself. It was mad. I might just as well have said I had decided to go on the streets!"

7

A FEW weeks short of Christmas Cassie came to the conclusion that the Garsides had been born unlucky. First it was Miss Jean who came home with bad news, then it was her father. At the beginning of November he had started rehearsing for a new play. A wonderful part, Jean had told Cassie.

"Is it a nice play?"

"Not very."

"Won't it run?" Cassie was beginning to pick up a few of the phrases attached to this curious way of living.

"Shouldn't think so. . . . What a thing to say! Bad luck! Forget you heard."

Forgetting was no good. The day before the play was to open there was a bus strike. Not everyone who could buy a seat at the theater could afford to travel by taxi to sit in it. They opened to a half-full house and a disgruntled press. Although the strike was over in forty-eight hours, those were the important hours for Miles Garside and his colleagues. The play never recovered. It faltered along for a couple of weeks and then the notice went up.

"Now see what your old busmen did!" Cassie cried the next time she saw Len.

Len had been rather reserved and silent lately. Now he told her for the first time that he was not going to work on the buses any more. He had had his training and he had been six weeks on the job before being told he was unsuitable. He had been given a good chance. Cassie, who had thought the Garsides unlucky, felt unlucky in her turn. She thought, too, of her brother Jack. Were they all living in an unlucky time so that nothing very good was to be expected?

It was a Sunday, Cassie's Sunday off, and they were walking as usual after Mum's good dinnner. Now Cassie wondered if it had been quite as good as usual—hadn't the meat been a cheaper cut? Certainly Dad had grumbled about a poor month's trade in October. Cassie and Len walked by the river and fog hung under the trees, blotting the color from the water and the sky. What if Mr. Garside and Miss Jean never got another job, and it came about that there was not enough money to keep and pay a living-in maid? Cassie had always supposed that people living in other places than the country had enough to live on, but now the picture of assured security began to blur.

"What shall you try for?" she asked Len.

"Alan's brother might get me something."

"Yes, but what?"

"He's got a good place at Smart's Engineering. Out Kingston."

"What's the job, though?" she insisted, perhaps unreasonably irritated.

"Storekeeper. Pay's not bad."

"Oh well," she said.

"Alan's got a good friend, Cassie. He was showing me how to ride his motor bike. Seeing I might need one. Seeing Smart's is right out along the bypass."

"All that money?" she cried.

"Alan'd get me one cheap. Secondhand. He's a good friend, Alan is."

"All right," she said. "Alan's a good friend."

They proceeded in silence which, though it was by no means unusual, yet seemed to threaten. Without looking at Len, Cassie began to wonder uneasily what she saw in him. He was kind and gentle, but it followed sadly that his kindness and his gentleness were bound up with a lack of push. He had had the intention of being a bus conductor without the ambition to make himself an acceptable one. That was partly his nature, so what it came to was a sheer lack of common sense in ever trying for the job. . . . As she began to think, Cassie became cruelly honest. What was the good of being a storekeeper? Where could that lead? He would be a storekeeper all his life. She felt a touch of real panic. She did not want to marry a storekeeper and she had often thought about marrying Len. Why had she ever thought of marrying him if she had known from the start he was unlikely to become a successful bus conductor? Because he had been the only boy to take an interest in her? It did seem very much like that. A couple of times he had taken her to dances in the same church hall where they had met. Everyone had acknowledged her as Len's young lady and they danced together, if you could call it that, practically the whole evening.

Now she glanced quickly at him as he walked beside

her, his tallness making him stoop a little, and seemed to
see for the first time that the mild blue eyes were a bit
empty, and the gently smiling mouth was set above a
slightly sloping chin. Cassie heard a tiny whimper of
disappointment sounding through her mind but almost
at once she began to feel fatally sorry for him. He was
disappointed by his failure, it was no moment to count
his shortcomings. Besides, hadn't she led him on a bit,
going out so regular and holding his hand in the pictures?
He had not plucked up courage to kiss her good night
so far—a good thing. In Cassie's world, though not in
Elsie's, a kiss, even in what Dad called these modern
times, was a promise.

"About Wednesday, Cass—"

"What about Wednesday?"

"That's when Alan's brother said I should go and see
Mr. Smart."

"Oh yes?"

"Four o'clock. I don't know how long I'll be. Better
call off the flicks."

She felt her heart jump a bit. What he had said was
sensible enough—he might not be back in time. Yet she
felt again the hint of doom. She had been asking herself
what she saw in him and had given herself little in the
way of a reply. It was not very nice, however, to consider
that he could all the time have been thinking the same
about her and considering his release.

Their walk had taken them in a circle and now they
were passing through the graveyard where Cassie took a
short cut from Dad's to Stanton Avenue. Here the fog
wreathed very suitably, and by now the dark was down.

She had not lately come this way herself, but had traipsed the longer way round by the brewery. Entering the place now, she felt again the familiarity of country-lingering things. They were lit by the fog-muffled glow of a street lamp at either end of the path—the grasses grown tall against the hedge and falling forward as they withered, the yews needing clipping as never at home at this season of the year, the arching stems of dog-rose from which the leaves were gone though the hips stayed bright and clustering. The smell of the damp earth might be the smell of any churchyard, but to Cassie Martle it was the smell of remembered times, of places where she had walked with other boys than Len. . . .

There was a little swing gate out of the graveyard. It was a kissing gate, but probably only Cassie knew it as that. Of its nature, however, the one moving through first coming face to face with whoever followed, it named itself.

"Cassie," said Len, catching her arm.

"Now what?"

That should have daunted him, but surprisingly it did not. Perhaps her own feeling of threatened change had infected him. "Give us a kiss, dear. . . ."

"Not now."

"Why not?"

"I might have a cold coming."

"Is that all? Come on—do!"

"Now now!" she said again, sounding pettish rather than sharp, giving him a chance, really, if he cared to take it.

"Cass. . . ."

"Oh do give over, Len. It's time I got back."

"Don't you want me to kiss you, then?" She thought he sounded rather hopeful.

"No, I don't. I don't feel like it. So that's that."

He let her go and she moved on her way. As he followed, the little gate closed with a sad defeated click. They walked in silence the rest of the way, and as they had gone a longer way round than usual it was a long silence. As was customary, he said good-bye outside Dad's and she went indoors and had tea before returning to the Garsides. She felt awful. She felt awful all the rest of the time, and awful when she got back to Stanton Avenue. The kitchen, which often seemed to welcome her now that she had set her own mark on it, appeared bleak and chilly.

Cassie looked with malevolent suspicion in the direction of the stove, which was frequently sulky and sometimes downright evil-tempered. She opened the front and all was black. She bent right down, setting her ear as near the bars as possible, like anyone else listening hopefully for a heartbeat. There was a very faint sound, like a mouse scratching in its sleep. The patient lived, if precariously. She began with the utmost tender care to riddle out some ashes. The mouse awoke. Cassie smiled grimly. There was always enormous satisfaction in getting the better of the stove. Even in her present mood it made her feel a lot more cheerful.

Mrs. Garside heard the riddling and came from the sitting room, asking as usual if she had had a good day.

"Yes, thank you," said Cassie, also as usual. She had noticed that she called Mrs. Garside "madam" rather less than she had done in the early days at No. 15—not because she felt any less respect for her employer, but because she had come to feel more respect for herself.

"I'm going up to bed now, so I'll say good night. The others are out. I've had a nice quiet evening on my own."

"Fancy!" said Cassie; for indeed it was unusual.

"Miss Jean and her father have gone to a theater. There are societies, you know, that produce plays on Sunday evenings."

"Oh?" said Cassie, amazed once again at what went on. "On Sundays!"

"Well," began Mrs. Garside. Then she stopped, unwilling, perhaps, to be drawn into any defense of such goings-on. "You might just cut a few sandwiches for when they come in, Edith."

"Yes, I will. Good night, then."

Mrs. Garside was at the door. She was carrying her library book, and also one of the thick pads on which Miss Jean wrote whatever she happened to be writing besides her diary or journal, or whatever she called it. Mrs. Garside paused at the door, hesitated, then decided that this was the moment to say something she must say. Cassie moved slightly so that she stood by the table, which then hid the new shoes she was wearing. Mrs. Garside had probably noticed them already, however. Cassie steeled herself for that faint reproach: "*More* new shoes, Edith?"

"Edith, I want you to help me," Mrs. Garside said. "We need to economize as much as possible at the moment. I know you understand. Will you take great care not to be extravagant or wasteful—don't use too much of anything, and see the hot tap isn't left running. All those little things make a big difference to the bills, you know."

This time Cassie answered quickly and warmly, "Oh yes, madam, I will. I will be careful."

"Thank you. I'm sure I can count on you." Mrs. Garside smiled and went away. Cassie heard her go upstairs and pause at the little boy's door. Then she went in and stayed a moment or two. As if he were still quite a baby, Cassie privately thought; but she knew enough of Roddy by now to know he would grow up in spite of them. Anyway, Mrs. Garside was a fairly old mother for so young a son, and maybe she should be allowed to fuss. And tonight she might be bothering about things like school fees.

The awfulness about Len left Cassie. She forgot him. She was drawn into other misfortunes and she would be happy to become part of them and try to help. She knew the Garsides were not wealthy because of the things they did not possess—you might expect them to live in a larger house, for one thing. People were buying cars nowadays, like that Mr. Lincoln, for instance, but it seemed unlikely that the Garsides would be able to do so.

So far from despising Mrs. Garside for speaking as she had, Cassie admired the straightforward, modest way she approached the business. She had not ordered but appealed, she had asked for help rather as Marge had done in Jack's behalf. The same sort of appeal would have been made to her own daughter—Don't leave lights burning, don't take more butter than you need, try not to have such huge baths. . . . This plain good sense was very far from the fierce, in-turned pride that Cassie had learned from childhood. Yet the two were sisters. . . .

"A very odd thing is that if D. and I go out together—like Sunday—we never quarrel. I really like being with him, he looks so good, and at Sunday productions he knows everyone, so I enjoy that, too. The only disagreement we had was about the play. It was marvelous. It was marvelous. He couldn't stand it. People go to the theater to enjoy themselves, he said. It's about *life*, I said. Well, they can get plenty of that any day of the year, my dear. . . . There was no quarrel about this because you have to *meet* to quarrel. It was like shouting to someone across a railway line—he was on the down platform, I was on the up.

"Still, there had to be something. When we got home I was still feeling chock-full of the play, and how real, and how well acted and everything. Then I had to think about how I had left M. my first three chapters to read. She had gone to bed when we got back, but she was sitting up reading when we both looked in on her. He sat down on the bed and took her hand very lovingly, and I hung about in the doorway.

" 'How was the play?' she asked.

" 'Oh—a morbid affair,' he said.

"(The lead was a sweet little man driven by his respectable wife to put his head in the oven. It was *real*.)

" 'I didn't find it morbid,' I said.

" 'I daresay not,' M. said, 'judging by what you gave me to read.'

" 'Didn't you like it?'

" 'I couldn't believe it was you writing. The deliberate —Why do you want to write of such things? Why can't you write pleasantly?'

" 'What's pleasantly?'

" 'Not like this,' she cried, pushing the MS across the eiderdown as though it smelled or something. 'Now don't lose your temper, Jean. Edith's left some sandwiches for you. You'd better go and eat them. And make some coffee.'

"Never felt less like losing my temper. You can't really shout and sob when you are experiencing despair. I picked up the MS and felt that I loved it, I hugged it.

" 'Good night,' she said, as if she had forgiven me. . . .

"I absolutely *ravened* in the night as I went straight to my room and skipped the sandwiches. . . .

"The Lincolns live where I can see their house. I found that out by accident. Sometimes in the night I wake up and go and hang out of the window. I've said that already, and about the trains. I can still see the railway because they have started building the next road from the other end. Three or four nights ago I was at the window, and the street lamps were still on. Houses and houses away there was a baby crying. No one went to comfort it. Just then the street lamps went out, but a house at right angles, a bigger and older house, had its lights on, and just then a car stopped outside. I don't know why I had to wait for the car to recognize the house, I've been there often enough and I am constantly looking out of the window. Then the downstairs lights were switched off, and one upstairs went on. The light showed up the pattern on the curtains—catching out Mrs. L., who always talks as though everything is lined and interlined and the *best*. . . . That's Anthony's room, that one over the porch, so there I stayed, and the baby still cried, and any minute I should cry, too. Everything seemed to be tied up, somehow.

"When they start building at the other end I shall lose the view of that house.

"Anthony turns up quite often during the evening and at weekends. If I get a job I shall only see him at weekends. He is very funny and makes me funny—he is a good audience. I don't really want a job. Perhaps it is all a mistake—the theater, I mean. There's that wonderful moment when the curtain swishes and the footlights blind you and the faces of the audience blob the dark behind. . . . All the same, it could be even better to see what you have written actually printed on pages and done up inside covers and with a beautiful jacket and your name. You would see it in the windows of book-shops. And of course the reviews. 'A book like no other I have read. . . .' That could mean whatever you wanted it to!

"Anyway—Anthony. He is not at all the sort of man I expect to like. I am inclined to admire actors who are rather D.'s type—which is a joke when you think how we row. Anthony is *plain*. He has hair of no particular color and he is not particularly tall, and with his rugger-broken nose (?) he likes to drink beer. I don't mean he *drinks*. His brother, John, is better-looking and very sophisticated. He works in the City—whatever that means. He has a girl called Penelope he might be going to marry. I fear Anthony has many girls and I am just one. Hopeless love has its compensations. (? Is that merely a quotation from everybody?) Melancholy makes me write—so that is one of the compensations. Perhaps if you're wildly happy it is too much trouble to write? Mrs. L. is frightful to Penelope, she does everything to make her look small —even to saying her petticoat is showing. She leads the poor girl on into expressing some opinion and then gives a crushing laugh. She is very nice to me. She favors me at the moment. Because she thinks I would be a meek daughter-in-law? Or because she knows she has nothing to fear of that sort? I am getting quite subtle in my ideas lately.

"Four of us went for a walk—John and Penelope, Anthony and me. It was very warm for the end of November—muggy. There are places on the common that are warmer than others—you move into gusts of it and then out again. I said it was thermal risings—I'm not sure what they are, but I read something. Anthony laughed, but it sounded rather good. He said if they were rising what were they doing between five and six feet from the ground, and I said the feet were the risings' feet. It is amazing how such remarks sound funny at the right moments. After a bit, John and Penelope got lost in the darkness. Did they walk faster or did Anthony walk slower? This is important. It is one of the subtle bits. But perhaps I am not clever at all about people, only suspicious? (I wish I didn't look round the other side, always. Whatever anyone does lately it is said to be because they have an inferiority complex. Perhaps I've got one. Would that make me pry and sniff at everything? I bet it would. How sickening.)

"The common looks marvelous when there is a full moon—the shadows are purple. . . . I am not writing this at all well, it is more like a schoolgirl's diary than a proper journal for posterity. *Purple* is simply not good enough. Once a girl at school, who was rather daring, said: 'When he kisses me all my purple passion rises.' . . . In fact the shadows are more a kind of crimson.

"That night—it was last night, actually—Anthony kissed me for the first time. I don't think I kiss very well. Still, I feel a bit of triumph. I feel that something has happened and now everything else could happen. I love him. I have never written that before except in stories. . . ."

"That Mrs. Lincoln!" said Elsie. Cassie was sitting with her at the Richardsons' while they were out playing bridge. "She's a madam all right!"

Cassie shrugged. She did not care at all for Mrs. Lincoln but she felt it was none of Elsie's business to comment, one way or the other. The Lincolns were friends of the Garsides; the Richardsons knew them, in Cassie's eyes, by chance. It was the chance of association at bridge afternoons, bridge evenings, or even bridge morning-into-evenings. The Garsides did not play bridge. Miss Jean had once remarked that her father was a wizard at poker and ought to make a good gambler. She had said he had all the instincts without the courage; whatever that was supposed to mean.

"There's nothing Mrs. Lincoln doesn't know," Elsie went on, "from making cakes to running the world—oh yes, she could run the world, all right. I pity any who marries those sons of hers."

Elsie was inclined lately to pity anyone married or likely to get married. Cassie knew this was because she had lost Alan—not that she had ever had much of a hold —and so far there was no one to take his place. The situation was aggravated by the fact that her younger sister, who worked in an office, had just got herself engaged. Cassie had often thought of asking Len to find Elsie a partner so that they could go dancing in a foursome. Elsie had found Len for her and now it seemed only fair that she should find someone for Elsie, but so far Len had not been at all helpful.

"Len's got a new job, then, Cass?"

"That's right."

"I never thought he'd be one for the buses."

"You were right, then, weren't you?"

"Out on the big road, is it, where he works? It's miles. How's he get there?"

"Seeing he hasn't bought his limousine yet—"

Elsie gave her wild laugh. "He could bike."

"That's a long way to pedal."

"Don't be so soppy! I mean a motor bike."

Cassie did not answer. She greatly feared Len's oft-proposed motor bike. He had been in the new job a fortnight, and the pay was not so bad after all. She had relented slightly in her estimate of him as a weak-willed boy barely worthy of her consideration. By now she had grown fond of him again, though in a rather mild, almost sisterly fashion. It was a depressing emotion for a girl of her age—seventeen, now, having had her birthday last week.

Cassie had been careful not to speak of the birthday at No. 15, but on the morning there had been a whole handful of cards from home. There was even one from Jack. Perhaps he had bought it out of the ten shillings she had not yet managed to repay. Still, what he could have spent on himself he had spent on her, which was nice. Mrs. Garside had noticed the cards and discovered about the day. She had gone shopping during the morning and had come back with a lovely box of soap and talcum powder. Miss Jean had given her a present, too—a pair of fur-backed gloves. "They look expensive," she had said hastily, "but actually they were given to me by some idiot who never found out the right size." Young Roddy had come into the kitchen when he returned from school and handed over a tin of toffees. He and Cassie had hugged one another in a pleasing way. Like his sister, he always said *Cassie*, never *Edith*.

Now, when they were together, Elsie and Cassie spoke of Christmas.

"Mrs. Richardson's having a children's party Boxing Day," Elsie said. "Then there's old Mr. and Mrs. Richardson coming to stay. I'll be run off me feet. What's your lot doing?"

115

"I don't think they know, not much. Mr. Garside's rehearsing again—opens Boxing Day. Then Miss Jean's got a friend coming."

"I'm glad to hear it. She doesn't seem to get much fun, with that Anthony Lincoln making eyes, and no job and everything."

"She's got her writing. She's very cheerful just now. Her and her mother are laughing about the place the whole time."

"Well. Fancy. Who's this friend?"

"Miss Anne Dennison. At school together."

"What's she like?"

"How should I know? I never saw her yet." Cassie then relented and admitted that she had seen a snapshot.

"Pretty?"

"A bit."

8

JEAN'S FRIEND, Anne, had been coming to spend the week before Christmas, but Jean developed flu and the visit had to be put off. It was agreed that she should come after Christmas, on the day after Boxing Day. The Lincolns were giving a party, so she was invited.

"You did say she was pretty, Cass?"

"I said she was a bit pretty. The snap's rather blurry."

"We'll see, then, won't we?"

It was obvious what Elsie meant, and who would not have meant the same? Cassie was not prepared to be a party to any insinuations, so she said that Miss Jean had a new dress and looked very nice in it; it was green.

"I'd never wear green, Cassie! It's unlucky to wear green! She's never going to wear green to that party?"

"You can be unlucky without you wear green," said Cassie firmly.

This exchange took place as Cassie and Elsie made their way to the church hall for the Christmas Bazaar. Elsie had Philippa with her, Cassie was in nominal charge of Roddy, now on holiday. But he and Bruce had rushed on ahead. Mrs. Garside and Mrs. Richardson were both helping at the Bazaar—Mrs. Richardson was running the baby-clothes stall, and Mrs. Garside was selling homemade cakes and pots of jam and fudge done up nicely in little flat boxes.

"Well, Edith?" cried Mrs. Garside. "Are you going to be a customer of mine?"

The hall was bustling full, its noise was cheerful, holly and ivy and green branches decked it rather tastefully; there were no vulgar paper chains or tinsel. Cassie smiled at Mrs. Garside and delighted in the feeling that they knew one another very well and were meeting here as friends.

"What shall I buy?"

"The fudge is delicious. It would make a good Christmas present. How about it? The boxes are so pretty, aren't they?"

They were. Some clever person had cut out pictures and pasted them on the box lids—last year's Christmas cards, Cassie decided, before Elsie saw fit to enlighten her —and then tied the boxes with gold thread.

"I'll tell you what," Mrs. Garside said, being helpful, "here's a box with a small dent. You can have it for a shilling instead of one and six."

"Oh. Yes. Thank you," said smiling Cassie, privately despising the dent. How could you give dented fudge for a present?

As it was a Saturday afternoon there were a lot of children dashing and bashing about the hall and being called to order by exasperated helpers. The Richardsons' Philippa, who was now walking nicely, had been given a little shopping basket to bring to the Bazaar. It was some time before anyone noticed her quiet progression from stall to stall, her absorbed choice and removal of suitable objects to fill the basket—a stuffed mouse, a pencil sharpener, a bar of chocolate, a cube of bath salt.

Miss Jean was looking after the hoopla. There had been a lot of talk about this at home, a lot of furious refusal and argument. The flu attack had seemed a possible escape, but Jean had made an effortless recovery. Now that the day had come, she was being so good at the task that Cassie concluded she must be playing the part of the hoopla helper rather than actually being one. She was very merry. She called out loudly to people. She chinked money in one hand. With the other she held the hoops, rattling them up and down like wooden bracelets from her wrist to the crook of her elbow. She shouted out, "Walk up! Walk up! Two a penny, five for tuppence!"

Cassie watched her in admiration. Perhaps she was wrong about the acting. Perhaps Christmas Bazaars were what Miss Jean and her mother really enjoyed—they both looked so easy and pleased with the obvious success of the afternoon. Suddenly their real world seemed to be their false world. It was as if one of those painted cloths they hang at the back of a stage had been rolled up, and beyond hung, not another picture, but a whole open prospect of simple things, ungilded, unlit, unpainted. Perhaps it was this that made Miss Jean so keen about "the country," nagging away with her questions in that curious, longing way—as if she had at some time been turned out of the place she loved and knew no way of returning. Although Mrs. Garside wore a smarter hat, she looked this afternoon like any of a score of lady helpers Cassie had watched at such functions as this one in her own village. She wondered for the first time how Mrs. Garside had come to marry an actor, and supposed they must have been very young at the time and too young to imagine how things might turn out. . . .

"*No*, Roddy!" Miss Jean was shouting. "Stop it! If you want any more rings you've got to be handicapped. Anyone winning more than three times must stand further back. A yard. A yard back for every prize ringed!"

Roddy shouted back. "You can't make up new rules!"

"Can't I? Can't I, just!"

People were laughing, but the brother and sister were furious and anger was quite unsuited to the occasion.

At this noisy moment Cassie watched Mrs. Lincoln arrive. She was a tall lady, inclined to sail, her hair white and curling and pretty, her face pretty, too, if you caught it wearing the right expression. Even with the rumpus round the stall, Cassie saw that Miss Jean was instantly aware of her. Anticipation was checked when she realized that the accompanying son was not the wonderful Anthony, but his brother. Still, the distraction was useful. Roddy and his friend Bruce removed themselves, melting silently into the crowd.

Mrs. Lincoln's commanding presence reacted on everyone else in much the same way. Jean lost her nerve, customers drifted away.

"I've brought John with me," Mrs. Lincoln was saying. "The Dutch auction. He's very good at running such things. I promised he should come. He always makes a lot of money."

"Now, Mother," said John. He looked pretty bored, Elsie said to Cassie.

"Anthony's still in town," Mrs. Lincoln said to Jean. "He promised to come. I suppose he's found something better to do."

"I suppose so," agreed Jean, falsely merry.

The hoopla board was almost cleared and she was able to stoop down and pull out the big box that held more prizes. She fumbled about among the tablets of soap, the packets of cigarettes, the bottles of hair cream, the packets of sweets. Either for sympathy or assistance, John Lincoln crouched down beside her.

"Give you a hand."

"Nothing very exciting left."

"There's another box, Miss Jean," Cassie said, eager to help. She pulled out a cardboard box from below the cloth that skirted the hoopla board.

"Oh—thanks very much."

Jean plunged her hand in the box. It was full of hand-knitted tea cosies. One after the other she pulled them out, plain colors, stripes, topped with crochet bows or crochet flowers, bulbous and soft and horrid.

"A species of hatting?" John suggested, clapping one on his head and one on Jean's. They began to laugh, standing up and solemnly bowing to one another. The damaged mood of a moment before was mended. The plain occasion, as vital to its protagonists as any meeting of a solemn board must be to the shareholders, regained its essential dignity.

"They're waiting to start the auction, John," his mother said.

"Coming, coming!"

"Do take that thing off your head. You look absurd."

"That's the idea, you see," he said. He turned the tea cosy back to front. "There! Now it looks rather more Dutch. Very suitable for the auction."

She stood waiting, as she might have done when he was a small boy defying her.

"Mother, really," he said, laughing only a little. He took off the cosy and tossed it to Jean. "Over to you, Miss Garside."

Cassie felt Elsie nudge her. She moved away, unwilling to take part.

"The Christmas Bazaar. I said I would never set foot on that ground but M. wheedled. She said everybody else's daughter would be willing to help—which did not encourage me. I really love her very much, though, and when we are singing in unison it is lovely. I have been singing because I am in love, and she has been singing because I am singing—though she is not at all easy about the being in love part. She tries not to think of any outcome, and as a matter of fact so do I. She likes Anthony but I know she thinks I can't see through him. Of course I can but it doesn't really matter. She does not want me hurt, but I know by now that it is much better to love hopelessly than not at all. Oh damn, that's only better-to-have-loved-and-lost—surely there must be *something* original to say, even about being in love?

"I was terribly, marvelously *good* about the Bazaar. I really tried. I tried like mad. I threw myself into it. The other daughters' mothers smiled on me. A thoroughly nice girl—after all. . . . And somehow I convinced myself that it was not too bad. Cassie was there. It's like the village, she said. Oh Cassie, thank you—it became like the village to me.

"The whole thing exploded when The Honourable Lady arrived with John in tow. Anthony found he had something better to do, she said; or words to that effect. John did his best, but she got the last word as usual. If all else fails to console me when Anthony removes himself to the Arms of Another I shall get a lot out of enjoying my salvation from Her.

"All the same—why should hoopla in a village be any nicer than hoopla in a London suburb? The people—the people must be realer. Cassie says their church hall—parish room, she calls it—is across the way from the enormous church that was built when that countryside was prosperous. (Must look that up—she could only say about it having been prosperous but didn't seem to know why.) When you come out of the church, Cassie says, you walk from the south porch down a long paved walk with yew trees on either side, and the graveyard is all about you. It is big, with generations tucked away, headstones of empty bones. If I die while I am still here in this place I shall have to be shuffled into some frightful row, and my raw white stone will be slotted in among the rest. Well—not raw and white forever, I suppose. But the tents in the recent encampments of the dead do seem excessively bleached. (?)

"To return to loving my mother: I didn't love her at all a couple of days ago. She picked up *Anna K.*, which I keep on reading, and unfortunately opened it at Kitty in childbirth. What a thing to happen after the words we had a few weeks ago over *Mother India*! But why does

she get only that kind of shock? I am forever reading Jane
A. but does M. pick up *P.&P.* or *Emma* and exclaim in
disgust at the social anguishes? Of course not. Both are
far away and long ago, but the physical matter is the
more improved. (I fear I read that somewhere. *T.&T.*?)

"Very early spring is best in their churchyard, Cassie
says. Then the ground is thick with snowdrops. . . .
Sometimes I think of going and staying in Cassie's village,
perhaps with two of my children, getting to know all the
family, being one of them.

"What nonsense."

Len seemed to like his job at Smart's big place. Cassie
decided she had better like it, too. But it narrowed her
whole vision in a way she could not possibly understand.
Why should it seem so splendid to think of him punching
bus tickets and so dreary to picture him in a brown
overall with *Smart's* on the pocket and a pencil stuck
behind his ear? There seemed very little reason in her
disappointment. But the picture she had had of him from
their first meeting had shown him swinging through
distant places like Putney and Wandsworth, crossing the
river into nameless excitements. Or on some differently
numbered route crossing the river in the opposite direction, careering along summer-leafy roads toward Twick-
enham or Isleworth, or to Chiswick via Kew. Now every
day he simply traveled to his own little cubbyhole and
stayed there until it was time to go home. She almost
hated him for liking it. She did not see herself as pigeon-
holed, because of the uncertainty, the variety, the contact
with a different world. Such things lent her life with the

Garsides a distinction she could never have imagined before coming to Stanton Avenue.

There was excitement now. Mr. Garside was rehearsing again, and feverishly, for the play that would open on Boxing Day. The play was a comedy, which would please Elsie. It pleased Cassie, for that matter. Miss Jean, however, seemed a shade reserved.

"The actor who was rehearsing the part has been taken ill. They had to get someone in a hurry. I hope it'll be all right. They're not a bit alike."

"Have he lots to learn?"

"Yes—*masses*! But he can learn quicker than anyone else in the world," Jean said, an unexpected pride in her voice.

In the evenings, when they were together in the sitting room and Roddy was in bed, Cassie would hear the strange murmuring of Mr. Garside learning his lines. Either Mrs. Garside or Miss Jean would be hearing him. Their lighter voices spoke a few words, then his came in. They "gave him his cue," so Cassie had learned. When she first heard the word she had wildly imagined they were playing some kind of a game, like Roddy's table football, only billiards. "Wait for the cue," one or other of the women would say. "Let me give you the cue again."

Sometimes it was as if they spoke a whole language among themselves. Once she had heard Mr. Garside say, "I dried completely and there I was right over by the O.P. corner." The *floats*, the *flies*, the *tabs* were all words of which Cassie would probably never learn the meaning. In a way, they were so fascinating in themselves she hardly wanted to.

Mrs. Garside had not actually suggested that the time for economy was over since her husband was working once more. Probably she was no more sanguine about the venture than her daughter, though she would never have said so. However, plans for Christmas seemed quite comfortable.

Cassie had a present for every member of her family. It was Mrs. Garside who found a big cardboard box for her and watched as she stowed the gifts away—the knitted mitts for Gran, the soap for Queenie, the pincushion for Marge, the calendar for Leslie and Katie, the propelling pencil for Jack, the chocolates for Amy. She was Cassie's least favorite sister, she hardly ever bothered to think about her; in fact Amy was loved properly only by Marge.

"I nearly forgot this, Edith." Mrs. Garside produced a tin of fancy biscuits, the lid decorated with views of London. She looked at Cassie with a quick, half-hesitant smile. "Will that be all right, do you think?"

"Yes. That'll be all right," said Cassie. She really wished she might hug Mrs. Garside, as she often hugged Roddy. She heard how flat her words sounded and felt the very slight withdrawal that resulted. "That's Buckingham Palace!" she cried, to make things better. "They'll like that."

When the box had been swathed in brown paper, and addressed in several places, and the string made secure with purple sealing wax, Mrs. Garside offered to take it with hers to the post.

"What about the stamp? I don't know how much."

"Never mind that now."

Mrs. Richardson would never do that for Elsie, Cassie

thought. And what about that lot at the Grange, where Marge worked? You couldn't see Lady Gwen paying for somebody else's stamp; but then she wouldn't go to the Post Office with parcels, either. . . . Cassie looked up quickly from the last knot and its blob of wax. She smiled and so did Mrs. Garside. It was as though Christmas had already begun.

An evening or two later, Mrs. Lincoln telephoned and asked to speak to Jean. Cassie called her and she came fast. With the kitchen door half-open, Cassie was bound to listen. She heard Miss Jean's too-eager voice, and then her good-byes. In the course of those she called Mrs. Lincoln Mrs. Lincoln at least four times. Then she hung up and rushed into the sitting room. Her father had come in from rehearsal at about six, just as if he were a proper working man. Her mother, as Cassie knew, was trying a gray school pullover on a fidgeting Roddy.

"They're going to the pictures and I'm going too."

"Who?"

"The Lincolns, of course! Can we have supper early?"

"Do stand still!" Mrs. Garside said to Roddy.

"Well?" Jean demanded.

"Well what?"

"Can we? Can we? Can we eat early? Otherwise I'll be late. It's only the big picture. They'll pick me up at half past eight."

"Yes, yes—don't get in such a state. Tell Edith."

Increasingly Cassie fussed about Jean and her Anthony Lincoln. If only she would keep calm. She reminded Cassie of Katie when she was after Leslie—overdoing it

127

most shockingly. She got him, but in Cassie's opinion only because he was so soft. He should've had more pride. Any boy ought to see that if one girl was so keen that she showed it—there'd be plenty of others he could choose from. In Cassie's mind a whole structure of laws about courtship had been building since she was eleven or so and it was unthinkable that she could easily throw down that structure and build it again in a different way. Miss Jean was breaking Cassie's rules the whole time. No good could come of it. No good *would* come of it and Cassie knew that already even if Miss Jean did not. Cassie knew that if anything had been likely to develop on Mr. Anthony Lincoln's side the signs by now would have been easy to read. It was Christmas next week. They had first become friendly in the summer. That was too long and already, as if on Jean's behalf, Cassie was bidding farewell to Mr. Lincoln.

A little after half past eight, sure enough, the bell rang and Miss Jean, who was upstairs, immediately started slamming drawers and rushing. Cassie went to the door in her best parlormaid's manner. It wasn't even the wonderful Anthony, but his brother John, with Mrs. Lincoln waiting at the gate.

9

WHILE CHRISTMAS was just being Christmas, Cassie took it
as it came and hardly had time to think about it. But
when it was over she knew it to have been the strangest
Christmas she had lived through. That was not only
because everything was different here in Stanton Avenue,
but because she had somehow experienced two of everything. There had been her own Christmas, which in itself
had been enough for any one person—and there had been
Miss Jean's.

The program had been a strenuous one. Cassie was
to work on Christmas Eve, when No. 15's turkey and
everything must be brought to table, but she would have
the whole of Christmas Day free. Elsie was working both
days and having Boxing Day off. That was Mr. Garside's
first night and his wife and daughter would naturally be
going. Mrs. Richardson had kindly invited Roddy to stay
that night and the next, which was the night of the
Lincolns' party. Cassie was to deliver Roddy to the
Richardsons' and spend the evening with Elsie. She would
also be going, in a roundabout way, to Mrs. Lincoln's
party, as she had been asked to go and help the Lincolns'
Jessie with the supper. It was quite a whirl. Cassie had
made herself a kind of diary of events, writing them on

the calendar in the kitchen, which now had very few leaves left to tear off.

"I wouldn't want to help her out," Elsie said, on hearing of Cassie's commitment to Mrs. Lincoln.

"Jessie's nice."

"Doesn't live in, though, does she? I bet not! Not seeing Mrs. Lincoln takes such care of her boys."

It was true that Jessie went daily to the Lincolns, but Cassie did not confirm Elsie's suspicions since she felt they reflected in some extraordinary way on Miss Jean.

Christmas Eve was the usual scramble of preparation, with even the twelfth mince pie of every dozen assuming a breathless importance. The postman kept coming—every hour or so, it seemed; a genial man who entered into the excitements, crying, "Nothing for you, young feller-me-lad!" every time Roddy went hurtling to answer the double knock that meant parcels.

It was nice for Cassie that everyone had packed a separate parcel, instead of making one big box, as she had done. Also they sent cards, quite separately—Leslie's crying, "What ho!" and Gran's in shaky writing, "God bless my girl." Cassie counted them over and sifted them through, and set them up on the kitchen mantelpiece. There were seven cards. She had supposed there might be eight, though she pretended she had not thought of this. Then Len made eight by sending the three kings struggling through an immense snowstorm, even though there was the star in the sky as expected—perhaps that was all part of the mystery. Cassie was pleased to have another card, though it was not the one she had looked for. She wondered a shade uneasily, however, if a card was all she should expect from Len.

Elsie came round with Bruce and Philippa and presents from the Richardsons and collected what the Garsides had for them. It was a curious business, when you came to think of it.

"Guess what, Cass?"

"What?"

"I got a card from Alan."

"Go on."

"Really! What'll I do? Send him one?"

"It'll never get there in time. Anyway—that will make him swollen-headed if you do. No boy deserves a card who's acted the way Alan has."

"That's right," agreed Elsie. But she sounded unconvinced and Cassie knew she would send the card, however she was advised.

"Len sent three wise men. What'd Alan send?"

"A sort of lantern with holly and words."

"What'd it say?"

"I haven't really read it yet—not the outside."

The Garsides, so Miss Jean said, usually saved up their presents for Christmas morning. But this year Mr. Garside would not be there—he had to dress-rehearse on Christmas Day, if you please, what a way to carry on. That was why the turkey was on Christmas Eve instead of at midday on Christmas Day, Roddy was to stay up and they would undo their parcels then.

"Keep your parcels, too, Cassie," Miss Jean said, "and open them with us."

"Well, I don't know what madam would say. . . ."

"She'd say it's a very good idea."

"There'll be the washing-up."

"We'll all do the washing-up."

"Oh dear," said Cassie. "I open them when they come."

"Do them up again."

"The paper's thrown away. . . ."

"You're hopeless!" cried Miss Jean, and stalked off, Cassie feared in a bit of a huff.

But Cassie would not have cared to open her presents publicly and have them exclaimed over. She had savored each one, as she had the cards, and had pored over them upstairs in her own room. Gran had sent a postal order for half-a-crown, and Jack, signing himself "Me and Sally," had chosen a comb and a powder puff in a little case—well, Sally had chosen that, no doubt, for Jack was working again and now they were engaged. Amy's present was a snapshot of them all taken outside the cottage, and it was done up in a frame she had made herself. Leslie and Katie, hard up with that obstinately growing family, had sent a snap, too. It was of all the children grouped round the latest lying in his pram. This time there was no frame, just a card folded round with a child's drawing of holly in the corner, and except for the baby they had all signed their names: Rita, Jeff, Dot, Peggy, Loretta; and Katie had written in "Kenny," for the baby. Marge's gift was best, it always was—a beautiful handkerchief sachet all embroidered, as only she knew how, with inside three hankies from Queenie.

It was a good haul, but the presents arriving for the Garsides from aunts and uncles and cousins and grandparents looked sumptuous even from the outside. Cassie would not have cared to set her own next to them. When the time came she just handed her own gifts to the Garsides, and still felt she was joining in. Mr. Garside gave her an envelope with an extra week's pay and she was spending it almost before she had finished thanking him. Mrs. Garside gave her a cap and apron. It was the prettiest ever, all done up in a beautiful gold box, but it was still a cap and apron. Miss Jean gave her a book, in spite of the fact that Cassie had read only three pages of the one she had been lent back in the summer, and then had returned it silently to the bookcase in Miss Jean's room.

"Oh," Cassie said now, "that's a dear little book!"

"It's poetry. It's about the country."

Cassie read out, "*A Shropshire Lad*," pausing briefly at Shropshire.

"I wish it was 'A Suffolk Lad,' Cassie."

"Well, he couldn't know, could he, Miss Jean."

They both laughed at this joke, and then Jean opened what Cassie had handed her. It was the cat-shaped bottle of scent, done up in yellow crepe paper.

"That's Pusskin," Cassie explained, smiling.

"Oh. . . ." Miss Jean opened, then closed, her mouth, "So it is! Look, Mummy—it's—it's—*Pusskin!*"

Cassie saw Mrs. Garside laughing, too, and she knew there was a little joke between them, but it was not a joke to be bothered about.

"He's lovely, Cassie. He's lovely! *Thank you!*"

"Hope he smell all right," said Cassie.

This time they all laughed together, Mr. Garside as well, his big voice booming out. Roddy, wearing the pullover Cassie had knitted, at which everyone had very pleasingly exclaimed in admiration, flung his arms round Cassie and dragged her under the mistletoe to kiss her. Then husband and wife kissed one another. There was no one just then for Miss Jean and she went out of the room, but she was still laughing. She came back seconds later, wearing a black velvet mask and a red paper hat out of a cracker. She carried a wand with a tinsel star at the top. In the doorway she paused and struck an attitude, holding her wand up in one hand, while in the palm of the other she held a torch concealed which she shone on her face.

"Now one and all get ready and prepare—
Behold the loaded board, the festive fare!
One hour more shall solve the oft-posed question—
Which of the family gets indigestion!"

They were mad, Cassie thought, as she ran giggling to set about dishing up the turkey. But nice mad.

Len had been invited to Christmas dinner at Dad's. He was already there when Cassie arrived. Dad had brought in a bottle of sherry and they had their glasses already in their hands. Mum was drinking ginger wine, so Cassie said she'd have some of that. It was immensely, splendidly ginger and caught the back of her throat like some terrible flame. There were cries of "Cough up!" and "Easy does it!" and when she recovered they all raised their glasses and cried, "Merry Christmas!" Dad clapped his arm round Mum, saying, "Give us a kiss, old girl!" and Cassie waited, wondering whether Len would do the same. And so he did, belatedly, urged on by Dad, by now a little merry. It was not much of a kiss. It wasn't as if she had to thank him for a present. A shade ladylike, she offered him her cheek.

Dad cried out, "Now then, Len! Don't let that do, bor!" falling back into the language he had been born with.

"Leave be, now." Mum said, just that much impatient. "I want Cassie in the kitchen. Come along, dear. There's still a lot to be done."

It was almost three o'clock before everything was ready, and then Dad opened the kitchen door and shouted, "The King!" They sat down together and listened dutifully, but the very instant His Majesty came to "God bless you all," Mum and Cassie were flying back to haul the turkey to the table, and the ham, and the bread sauce and everything else that went with such a meal. If things were tight, if trade was bad, there was going to be no hint of it at Christmas time. . . .

Later, Cassie and Len went for the walk they always took when he came to Dad's. They went in the darkness now along the riverside and saw the lights reflected in long waving streamers that almost met in mid-stream. The tide ran here, but all was totally silent, the holiday not yet over, everyone at home, the presents given and received, the feasting surely flagging. Len took Cassie's hand as they walked, and they talked now and then, but Len had never a great deal to say. When they passed under a street lamp they looked at one another and smiled, but vaguely.

Tonight, as usual, they parted when they got back to

Dad's. Len had been asked to stay, but he had promised his sister he would be back before the children went to bed. Uncle Len. This was a guise in which Cassie had never considered him. In a curious, faint way she felt jealous.

This time they kissed on parting, but it was a warm and friendly kiss, passionless and comfortable and without promise. Cassie watched him down the road and when he turned at the corner she waved. Then she went indoors.

She heard voices as she closed the door behind her— Mum's, Dad's and another, Dad sounding surprised and pleased. Cassie went into the little parlor, hearing him say, "Well, would you believe that! Well, here's a fine thing! All the way to London! Would you believe that? Wait'll our Cassie come in."

She said, "I'm here."

She looked across the room to the visitor, who rose slowly.

"Hullo, Cassie."

"Hullo," she said. "Hullo, Ned."

"Mr. Clare," Ned explained. "He give three days and my train money. I come to visit Rosie."

Rosie was his sister who had married a foreigner and settled with him, therefore, in his native London. Mr. Clare was the farmer Ned worked for.

"That fare to me wholly kind," said Cassie, carefully.

"Seeing that's the first Christmas since poor Mother went. He said."

Indeed it was kind, they all agreed, Mum expanding on the matter, Dad nodding, Cassie silent.

"Old Mrs. Martle say for sure to see out how their Cassie's doing. How are you, Cassie?"

"Quite well, thank you."

Across the room they gazed at one another. He's older, she thought. But she was older, too, and the change in her was almost certainly greater than the change in him. She was wearing her newest dress, special for Christmas, blue, but rather tight and with a neck Mum thought too low but knew better than to mention—though her glance had been enough. She was wearing also real silk stockings and shoes with straps and high heels.

"You look a little strange," he said.

Mum said that was what came of living in London. "Everyone's smarter in London."

"She speak different, too."

Cassie frowned. She had spoken twice only, and the first words had come out of her instinctively, simply at the sight of him.

Dad began asking about people at home, for though it was many years since he had lived there he remembered all the friends of his youth and his early manhood. Cassie sat very still, listening to the names, listening to the country creeping back into Dad's voice, listening to Ned's remembered tones, watching his face. He seemed to her handsomer than when she last saw him. His jaw had squared and he was very upright, his shoulders broad without coarseness, his face brown even now in the winter. Last summer's sun was stored in his skin and in the bones that stretched the skin. He looked what he was, a country lad in London, wearing his good suit and a bit wary of what might happen to him in such a place. Cassie did not know what she wanted to say to him, or even if she wanted to say anything. Once they had spoken of the family one by one there seemed nothing more she needed to know; at least, nothing she would ask about. She looked at her hands which, in emulation of Elsie, she protected in a number of ways from the ravages of housework— washing-up in rubber gloves, smoothing in cream, shaping and polishing her nails.

After the great Christmas dinner there was not much to be said for supper. Anyway, it was time for Cassie to get back to Stanton Avenue and for Ned to make his way back to his sister's place. In the early hours he would catch the workmen's train that carried railway mainte- nance men out of Liverpool Street. He would be home in time for mucking-out, though not for milking.

"You can walk our Cass home, then, bor," said Dad.

Mum said the first silly thing Cassie had ever heard her utter. "Whatever would Len say to that?" she cried.

Cassie said nothing, Dad laughed—and began advising about how Ned should get back to his sister's place. "There'll be a late bus or two, top of Stanton Avenue— Cassie'll show you. Anyway, holiday or not, there's al- ways carts going into Covent Garden. You'd get a lift easy. They pass near your sister's."

"Thanks, then," said Ned.

Cassie had sometimes woken in the night and heard the carts, wheels rumbling, hoofs clopping, the drivers nodding along the familiar route and maybe the horses, too, moving in their sleep. She liked to lie warm and comfortable, listening to the sound that was like home at the beet harvest—save that there the road was still soft and the wheels and the hoofs were quieter. . . .

"This way, is it?" Ned asked, as Cassie steered him round the corners and the short cuts.

"It's through the churchyard. Not afraid of ghosts, are you?"

He was not afraid of ghosts. Now Cassie chattered and Ned was silent. She spoke of whatever came into her head—the Garsides, Elsie, the shops in Oxford Street, wicked young Roddy and his friend Bruce. She went through the kissing gate ahead of him, but they came face to face as expected, and as expected he caught her gently and leaned toward her.

"What Len's that?"

"A friend."

"Shall I tell your Gran you're walking out?"

"No!"

"Come home, Cassie," he said, as Queenie had done, but quietly. "There's the cottage and only me."

"I'll come for my summer holiday."

"That's only Christmas yet."

She saw the months, unwinding and unwinding.

"Summer soon come," she said.

"Why are you different?"

"I'm all right."

"You were better before."

"Well, thanks, I'm sure."

"I think of you."

"Come on—I'll be late."

"Kiss me, then. You're still my Cassie."

"I don't want to. And I'm nobody's Cassie but my own."

She pulled away and went out of the gate, sharply flouncing; but under the street lamp he caught her up and grabbed her hand.

"I won't never forget you, Cassie. Think of that. . . ."

She could not answer, if she did she might cry. She did not know what she wanted, of him, of Len, of herself. But as he still held her hand she leaned against him, helplessly and hopelessly.

"I can't think, Ned. I can't think at all."

He put his arm round her and walked her on along the street, saying, "There. It don't matter all that. Not for tears."

In this way, she still struggling not to weep, they reached No. 15.

"This is it," she said.

She flung her arms around him, then shoved away before he could prevent her and ran off down the side way to the house. She bolted the door, and perhaps he might have heard that? She went into the kitchen and stood in the middle of the floor, trembling and feeling sick and giddy. When would she ever see him again, and why should she want to—a stupid country boy, too clumsy to be thought of, too ignorant to know about theaters and William Shakespeare and rehearsals. . . .

The house was quiet. Mr. Garside had not yet returned. There was a note from Mrs. Garside placed on the kitchen table: *Don't wait up. We have gone to the Rich-*

ardsons'. That would mean that Rodney would be staying there for one night more than had been arranged. It meant less work, but Cassie always missed him when he was away.

She went slowly upstairs to her room. The empty house did not trouble her, but there was an emptiness inside her that was both fear and pain. She undressed listlessly, hanging up her new dress with care and smoothing it as if she loved it, yet seeing it as something alien she had taken on herself—like the national dress of a foreign country. She stood in the slip and knickers that were a cheap version of Miss Jean's, and imagined many things— but came in the end to Gran's face if she could see them. She had no clothes from home now save a cotton petticoat that Marge had made for her and trimmed with lace. It had seemed very dainty and pretty when she left for London, but now it lay forgotten.

There was the sound of the front door opening and all the Garsides returned together, talking in low voices and laughing. It was their best mood and it remained with them until they all said good night. Their bedroom doors closed, Miss Jean's clicking close to Cassie's listening ear. She heard Mr. Garside saying something about the whole cast having been sent home by taxi. . . . Miss Jean thudded about for a bit, then her light went off. There was a spring in her bed that always pinged as she settled down.

Cassie settled down in her turn. After some time, lying awake, she heard the first carts moving along the main road.

Cassie's Christmas was now over. Miss Jean's had barely begun.

In accordance with the Garsides' usual indifferent fortune, the new play opened to a cool reception and a mixed press. On the breakfast table at No. 15 on the morning after Boxing Day there appeared a great pile of newspapers—*The Times, The Telegraph, The Morning Post,* which were the respectable ones; *The Daily Mail, The Daily News, The Daily Express* and *The Chronicle, The Daily Mirror* and *The Daily Sketch,* which were of a different rating; and, just for such occasions as this, *The Daily Herald.* The three Garsides divided this pile between them and the bacon chilled on their plates, the toast grew limp. In these papers were what Miss Jean had explained were *notices* of last night's new production. "When I write my novels," she had told an uncomprehending Cassie, "I shall get *reviews* in the papers; but when I play a part in the theater, I shall get *notices.*" It was all the same to Cassie, who would always call both "the newspaper pieces."

"Here's a good one!" Miss Jean was saying, as Cassie brought in more coffee. "*The Sketch.* Listen: 'Miles Garside displayed a gift for comedy of which his admirers, and they are many, have until now been unaware. And—' bla, bla, bla—'This gifted actor should be offered more opportunities to exploit this side of his considerable abilities.' There you are."

He only looked up from *The Times* and said to his wife, "What about *The Morning Post?*"

"Well. Not too good, alas."

142

"What's it *say?*"

"It's rather long. You read it later." She folded the paper firmly. "Have you got *The Mirror*, Jean?"

"I fear I have."

"Bad?"

"I've only got to the headline. It says: *What Next?*"

It needed no more for Cassie to understand that the household had not, after all, come to an end of their economies. As she left the room Mr. Garside was saying, "Well, that's that, I suppose. It was always a mad idea to open on Boxing Day. . . . I'm sorry, my dear."

"You never know. We've had bad notices before now and the play has still run."

"I laughed like mad," Jean said. "I thought everybody else was laughing. I suppose the critics were jaded after Christmas. I agree with *The Sketch*. I thought you were frightfully good and extremely funny. Can I have some tickets and take Anne?"

"I daresay it can be arranged."

He sounded calm, as was his way at such moments. Later he would concentrate on the notice in *The Sketch* and his daughter's comments. This, which Cassie could not possibly know, was the life-saving vanity of any actor; without it few could survive.

Now, Christmas having given way to the new play, the new play gave way to the arrival of Miss Jean's visitor.

"*Is* she pretty, like you thought?" Elsie would ask.

Cassie would have to answer, Yes and no, for she could not quite decide. She knew what Elsie would say about Miss Anne: "She's got IT," which Cassie thought very common. Or she would say "She has S.A., meaning sex appeal, which was not much nicer. Strictly speaking, the visitor was not pretty. There was that about her, however, which Cassie recognized all too clearly, and with a sinking heart.

"We played endless silly games," Jean wrote in her journal, though not until after Anne's visit was over and she had been waved away from Waterloo Station. . . .

"There was a new girl of John's, called Denise. Penelope has mysteriously vanished and was never spoken of. Denise had the best dress. It was black and chiffon and rather long, so mine felt very short. It had full bishop sleeves and the skirt was accordion-pleated. She is really rather nice, though. Mrs. L. was therefore pretty nasty to her, in spite of it being a Christmas party. For one thing she asked Denise if she was in mourning, thus making plain that girls, in her opinion, should wear pretty pastel shades. Then she turned her attention to me, tweaking at my skirt and calling it my 'frill.'

"Everyone was nice to Anne, who sat looking vague and saying nothing but getting all the attention in spite of it. (Because of it?) There was an old friend of Mrs. Lincoln's there, I think they had been to school together, just like Anne and me. She had a flowing dress of royal blue lace and wore her hair in earphones. Long ago, when I was small, M. wore her hair that way, and then one day she came back from the hairdresser's carrying two thick dark red plaits in a box. I reminded her as they started handing round the eats at Mrs. Lincoln's. 'It was the day I was emancipated,' she said. I was much surprised, partly that she should think she *is* emancipated. I know as little about her, I suppose, as she knows about me. There's no one in the world but strangers.

"The food was rather good and I kept making excuses to carry things into the kitchen because Cassie was there, looking reliable. I felt she was supporting me in some way.

"Anthony was in his nicest mood, which means he was funny with me and nice to his mother, who can at times drive him—though never John—to the blighting of a sociable occasion. After a bit we all sat round and played a game called Man and His Object, sort of Animal, Mineral, Vegetable, only in this one two people have to go out; which is good. John went out with Denise. He was Man and she (ha ha) was his Object. We chose an organ-grinder and his monkey. Denise was brilliant and guessed it in three. Mrs. L. then asked Anne, but she said she was no good, so they let her off 'for the time being.' So then it was Anthony and me.

"We went into the dining room and scraped up some of the remaining food. Anthony had a great bowl of apple fool and insisted on spooning it fast into my mouth. I knew I should splutter it down my dress, and of course I did. Fortunately the pattern more or less hid the marks. Anthony tried to clean me up with handfuls of paper napkins and was all for dipping one in the lemonade and washing my face. He must have been a bit drunk, but I don't know how unless he has secret bottles in his bedroom—the cup we drank at supper tasted about as strong as scented bathwater. Just as I thought he might set about kissing me—Mrs. L. knows better than to put up mistletoe—we got called in.

"This time I was Man and Anthony was the Object—which I didn't like much, as it seemed to have one of Mrs. L.'s hidden meanings, only less hidden than usual.

"A lucky thing happened. After the apple fool and all that dottiness in the dining room, I was in a wild mood. After the A., M., V. bit, which is inescapable, I asked, 'Do I pass me every day?'

"For some happy reason this threw everyone into convulsions. It was one of my biggest successes, though I am fairly famed for thinking up good questions. When they had all recovered a bit, someone said the answer was 'Yes,' so with unabated wit I said, 'Oh I know—the top of the road.'

"This drew cheers and a good round of applause, though it didn't mean a thing really. I saw M. watching me and being pleased because I was a success for once. Then Anthony tried and was very bad, but by that time everyone was in a mood of hilarious and idiotic good temper. It took a long time to guess that we were Gandhi and his begging bowl. That annoyed me, since Gandhi is no laughing matter, but I was enjoying myself too much to spoil it, and so, with disgusting treachery, I roared with the rest.

"Eventually, after the blue lace and Mrs. Lincoln, and M. with Mrs. L.'s brother, Laurence, there was only Anne left. I started praying that D. would turn up and break into the game because everyone then would be concerned about hearing how the play had gone on its second night, and the game would finish. But he was terribly late arriving. Anne got confused and pink and I could see both John and Anthony beginning to notice her rather a lot. At last Anthony seized her hand and pulled her to feet, saying nobly, 'Come on! For your sake I'll go through it again.' And out they went.

"One of the troubles about this game is that after a few rounds one gets so horribly bored and can't think of anything original or even sensible. The two who have gone out have to wait longer and longer while independent conversations start up among the rest. Anne and Anthony waited longer and longer. I started praying again—this time that Cassie and Jessie might now be clearing away the supper things and spoiling Anthony's chances. I knew Anne would hate it if he grew amorous; after all, we are such friends, and anyway she says she is practically engaged. But as I know Anthony has a leaning toward any girl, I knew he might try it on. Anne has something about her that beckons men to her side, apparently without her doing anything about it. I wish I knew what it is. It is definitely something I shall never have.

"Just then the doorbell rang and everyone exclaimed, and John went to the door and let in D. As it happened they had played to a good house and a marvelous reception, and he had got a round on his first entrance (he told us later), so he was in tremendous form and went round gallantly kissing hands. Mrs. Lincoln flushed unbecomingly, either because she liked it or because she didn't. The noise and everything broke up the awful game and Anthony and Anne came back. She looked across at me at once and I had a sudden frightful sinking feeling.

"Later we played cards—Rummy and things and finally Pontoon. Anthony and I usually play this together, sharing a hand. Anne said she didn't know how to play so Anthony said he would show her, they should share a hand. I sat on the opposite side of the table and tried to flirt with Uncle Laurence, who is a male Mrs. Lincoln, but an unmitigated and abominable *bore*—which she, in fact, is not; not a bore. Everyone was smoking and the air got thicker and thicker till I could hardly see across the table, and just as well. My eyes smarted so much I knew they must be bright red. I decided I was probably looking just about my worst."

Miss Jean's friend was sharing her room for the few nights of her stay. She had the bed with the singing spring and Miss Jean had a camp bed. Cassie heard the two of them talking long after the house was dark. She thought the door must have been left open—Miss Anne would have done that for she was, Cassie had noted, extremely casual, leaving everyone in a draft and dropping her handkerchief all over the place.

"Well, I'm sorry," Anne said at last, after a lot of rather angry but unintelligible talk. "I'm sorry, I tell you. But I couldn't help it, could I? He's obviously like that. He kisses anybody."

"You mean—he actually kissed you? You *let* him?"

"Well what would you expect? We were out there ages. We had to do something."

148

There was a long, long silence.

"What a fuss, Jean! What's a kiss?"

Cassie did not hear what Jean replied. But after a moment or two there was a determined opening and closing of the bedroom door. She heard Jean going downstairs. She went into the sitting room and again a door shut. Cassie guessed she had removed herself to spend the night on the sitting-room sofa. It had a let-down end and was really rather comfortable. Only Cassie wondered and wondered if Jean had been calm enough to take a blanket with her—Anne was using the eiderdown. She thought how she and Jessie had wondered if they should go into the dining room where Anthony and Anne were together, and clatter about taking away the remains of the food. But Mrs. Lincoln had said only to tidy up and leave fresh plates and forks, in case anyone wanted to help themselves; this had been done long before. So she and Jessie had remained gloomily in the kitchen, Jessie, very nicely, as much concerned as Cassie had been. . . .

Well, it was too late to worry about it now. It had happened.

10

"ON THIS day, St. Valentine, I Gave Up The Theater. Now that it is written down I feel better about it. I feel extremely relieved. First of all there were considerable rows, of course. Not because I was giving up but because everyone said I ought to, which made me mulish. You *must* get another job, they said. So easy, when there's nothing I've been trained to do and lots of quite brilliant people are out of work. Still, in two years I have only earned about twenty-three pounds, so it is sensible, really, to retire. M., of course, is glad, as she still suffers all kinds of deep-rooted dreads about my being swept into loose living. Chance is a fine thing! I don't know if D. is disappointed. I suspect he started being so years ago when he discovered he had no raving beauty on his hands, no perfect Juliet or glorious Rosalind. Actually, I could play Rosalind if I were given the chance. And Beatrice, forsooth—I know she ran like a lapwing, but they're quite large birds. . . .

"Something lucky happened to me, which is not usual in this family. I took Roddy to Kew Gardens on a Saturday morning, and on the way back in the bus I was looking out as we came into Richmond and saw a notice in a shop window, *Barty's Bookshop Opening Shortly*. It was too late to get off at that stop, but I leaped up and pulled the bell and it stopped a few yards on. Roddy looked dumbfounded. 'Please see he gets off at Stanton Avenue,' I commanded the conductor. Who for some reason thought I was funny and grinned as he promised. Anyway, Roddy knows perfectly well where to get off—I'm the one who sometimes gets carried past the stop because I'm thinking. I went straight to the shop, I had to do it while the fit was on me, and asked for a job. The place was full of books being unpacked and there were still workmen hammering at shelves. It was glorious.

"Barty is a little gray man, but he has a lively, slightly terrifying sister, who is obviously the one who will be running the place. There was a lot of talk about inexperience, but when they asked me questions about what I had read and what I liked reading I knew I was doing well. But it was so much easier asking for a job which had nothing to do with being or not being beautiful, that I gave a much better performance than any I have even attempted at an audition. At last they said if I would take £2 a week for the time being, until they saw how the shop went, then I could have the job. . . . Funny thing was that I went out in such a dream I left my gloves behind and had to go back for them. As I walked in I heard Miss Barty say in ringing tones, 'Anyway, she has such a very nice appearance—and I liked the bit about her academic qualifications. "I failed Junior Cambridge!"' She was laughing so much she never saw my re-entry downstage right and quick exit left.

"Well.

"Barty's Bookshop opens a week on Monday, nine till

six, but please be there by a quarter to nine (and leave at a quarter past six, I shouldn't wonder). Nine till twelve on Wednesdays. My bus fares will cost me sixpence a day, or I might walk half the way for the good of my health and strength. I can get lunch for a shilling or one and six at the most, or I might bring sandwiches from home. When it is fine I can go and eat my sandwiches sitting on a bench on The Green, or I can walk down to the river and sit there by the sliding water in bright and beautiful sunshine. Then there's my insurance stamp, just like Cassie's, I don't know quite how much, but I think about sevenpence halfpenny. But I am bound to have well over a pound left each week. Think how much Cassie buys on much less. . . .

"I believe Cassie has had a Valentine, but she hasn't said."

There was no name in Cassie's Valentine, but she knew who had sent it. It was not the kind you buy in a shop. It was three snowdrops pinned to a piece of paper among a scatter of dry moss. The paper was then folded and *Valentine* printed across it in green ink. The snowdrops, flattened as they were sped through the post, were still living when the envelope was opened. As she held them, their heads very slightly shifted, as though they had lived just long enough to accomplish their mission and could now peacefully expire. Cassie folded the Valentine into one of the handkerchiefs Queenie had given her for Christmas, and then put it safely into Marge's sachet.

"I thought you'd be awfully glad," Jean was saying to

her mother, when Cassie took in the tea tray.

"I am glad, Jean. Of course I'm glad, darling."

"You don't want me to work in a shop!"

Mrs. Garside shot a glance at Cassie and said quickly, "Don't be so absurd."

"Anyway, it's a bookshop. A *bookshop*! I shall be able to read and read."

"I should imagine you'll be there to work."

"There won't be customers all the time. I shall be able to read every book in the place in time."

Cassie, having set down the tray, was then obliged to exit without any hope of hearing what she now knew to be called "the curtain line."

"I said I shall be able to read everything in the place. 'I hope not quite everything,' she said. She said it sadly. It really is dreadful how narrow she is when she is also very nice. However, she's not as narrow as her sister. A good story was of cousin S. looking up from a novel that *I* had recommended—she was about fourteen—and asking, 'What's the difference between a wife and a mistress, this man seems to have both.' The heavens all but fell, so I was told. . . .

"It would be better if Barty's were further from home. I know why M. feels this and I understand. It is a lingering something from her girlhood. When she and her sisters were young they were obliged to work in their father's shop, measuring yards of silk and fitting the local ladies with doeskin gloves. They must have been a wonderful trio—one blond, one red, one dark. An old lady told me they were a sensation at dances and their programs

153

were always filled in the first ten minutes. So they would dance grandly under chandeliers in that great ballroom down there, and then the next morning, after something like the Yeomanry Ball, there they were back behind the counter. Classically fairy-tale, but no princes. M. told me that if they saw someone coming in who had been at the ball the night before, they would bob down and hide under the counter. They were 'educated above their station,' which made it, no doubt, more difficult for them, but has given me a start. One day I might write a novel about them, but as they must all die first I shan't think about it yet."

Life was quite changed once Miss Jean had started what Cassie could not help thinking of as a proper job.

"She leave eight-fifteen," she told Elsie. "So it's bang on her door half past seven and hope she stays awake. Then down she come and I give her her breakfast."

"Two breakfasts to get now, then. I must say!"

"That's no great burden. That's quite a pleasure."

"You're a softie," Elsie assured her, but in a tolerant voice that suggested it might be part of her charm. Elsie was a good deal easier-tempered these days, having renewed her goings-on with Alan. Elsie was the softie, so Cassie thought.

At breakfast those mornings, Cassie stayed to talk to Jean, leaning against the door, pretending she was just going back into the kitchen. What they talked about was nothing much—odd things Miss Jean liked to hear about country living, bits of gossip about the bookshop; and, on

Cassie's side, discussion of clothes, to which Jean was always ready to contribute. As soon as Jean had swallowed the last mouthful, crying as usual, "I must fly!" Cassie went back and had her own breakfast before starting all over again to get another on the table for the Garsides by eight-thirty. For all Mr. Garside got so late to bed, he was always up on time in the morning.

After some weeks of the new regime, Jean said, "Do sit down, Cassie. Why don't you bring your breakfast in here?"

Cassie was still, amazed. Then she said, "Madam wouldn't like that."

"She doesn't appear until after I've left."

"Well," said Cassie very slowly, "no. I don't think I care to."

"Then why don't I have my breakfast with you in the kitchen? That really would save time and trouble."

Cassie laughed. "No, miss. No, I don't think so."

"All right—if you want to be so stuck-up."

"I don't know what you mean."

She would not budge, for all Jean's blandishment. She continued, as the weeks went by and the season changed, to lean against the door while Jean had her breakfast in the dining room, then retired as usual for her own. Yet there was a change between them. The ground had shifted and they stood much nearer. When Cassie watched Miss Jean leave in the mornings she was already touched with the pleasant anticipation of her return. Jean, on her side, made a point of greeting Cassie in the kitchen each evening as soon as she had disposed of the "What sort of a day?" routine with her mother. . . .

One Sunday in early April, almost a year since Cassie started at No. 15 Stanton Avenue, she was at Dad's as was usual on her free Sunday and Len failed to appear.

"Muddled the date," Dad said. This had happened once before; Len had appeared the Sunday following, when Cassie was on duty.

"We'd best wait a bit," said Mum. "Then I'll just have to get dished up or the dinner'll spoil."

She sat down and talked of other things—Cassie's holiday, due and even overdue; had anything been said about it?

"Oh yes—Mrs. Garside tell me Thursday—they'll have three weeks this year. So I can have three weeks, too."

"She'll pay you?"

"Of course!" Cassie had felt no need to ask.

"Seeing his play's done so well, I suppose they're a bit flush."

"Miss Jean can't go with them, though. She's not been long enough at her job to get a holiday."

"She'll never stay in the house alone?"

"She would, only Madam won't let her. Mrs. Lincoln say she can stay there."

Mum looked pleased, knowing as she did every detail of Miss Jean's slender affair with Mr. Lincoln. "That's a very good idea, Cass."

Cassie pulled a face. "Only *he* won't be there. Him and his brother's going a trip to France."

"All the time?"

"So she tell me." Cassie corrected herself. "So she tells me."

After another fifteen minutes, Mum said she'd best get

the dinner on the table. "I daresay he's got the flu," she said, though not looking at Cassie as she spoke. They did not speak of Len again. When the meal was cleared away, Mum and Dad thought a nice walk would be the thing. It was quite strange, walking with them instead of with Len. They knew different short cuts, and they emerged at an unfamiliar part of the river, with old houses quite near the water, and gardens with daffodils and such.

"If so be you haven't saved your train fare home, Cassie, Dad and me'll help you. Won't we, Dad?"

"Oh yes. That'll be all right. I'll see you have your fare. Your Gran'll be glad to see you."

She said, "Thanks, Dad." And at once she saw herself in the train, how smart her clothes would look when she stepped out at the other end. Who would meet her at the station? She knew it could be Ned. She would try to catch a train arriving while he was still at work; she did not know quite why she decided this. Then it would be Leslie, who worked for himself and so kept easier hours.

When she got home that night, Cassie sat down at the table with its checked cloth, and wrote a letter home.

"Dear Gran. I hope you are well. Oh Gran it is come near my holiday only to August and I shall be home with you. Your loving Cassie." She read it through and thought it sounded a bit bold. "PS. That is, if you like that I come."

On the following Wednesday, Mrs. Garside took Mrs. Richardson to a matinee of Miles Garside's unexpectedly successful play. Jean was at home. The telephone bell rang and she sprang to it before Cassie could get there. It was Cassie's afternoon off but she had stayed in to finish a jumper she had knitted; she wanted to wear it to go to the cinema with Len—if he should turn up, she added with some sarcasm, though she did not suppose he would default twice running.

Cassie came into the hall just in time to see Jean lift the receiver, smoothing and tweaking at her hair just as if she could be seen from the other end of the wire. Then she said, "Oh. Yes. Wait a moment. Hold on." She looked back over her shoulder, the receiver pressed against her chest. "It's for you."

Cassie froze. Who would telephone her? Elsie had done so before now, but Mrs. Richardson had turned stuffy. Of course, as Mrs. Richardson was out this afternoon. . . .

"Come on, buck up!"

"Is it Elsie?"

"No, no—it's a man. Come on quickly."

Cassie eventually arrived to take the telephone from Miss Jean. She held it gingerly, as if she had no experience of such an enigmatic invention, though ordinarily she was rather brisk and clear when she handled it.

"Yes?" she said warily. "Oh. It's you, Len."

"Expecting someone else?"

"Not particularly."

"Sorry about Sunday, dear. My sister asked me there special. Stan's brother's home from Australia."

"That's nice."

"Look, Cass—I'm working late all this week. I can't help that, can I?"

"No, I'm sure not. You mean you're not coming this evening, either."

158

"Either" was a bit barbed and he paused while he swallowed it.

"That's right."

"See you some time, then," said Cassie; and hung up instantly, though without any clatter, just quietly cutting him off. "Fancy that," she said to Miss Jean, who did seem rather to have been lurking. "Very busy all at once."

"I've never seen you looking angry before, Cassie. What happened?" She said when Cassie explained, that she supposed he couldn't help it. "People do have to work late, after all."

"That's a likely story," Cassie said.

She went into the kitchen, bundled up the new jumper and shoved it into a drawer in the dresser, thudding it closed. She started banging about. Cupboard doors slammed, china rattled. She saw Miss Jean standing in the doorway watching her, trying not to laugh.

"What film is it this week?"

"Ronald Colman and Vilma Banky."

"Let's go, then."

"No thank you, miss," said Cassie, putting Jean firmly in her place. She could see that pleasing Madam—what a dotty suggestion—she would have thought Miss Jean might have more sense.

"Have it your own way," Jean said; she left the kitchen whistling that tune out of *The Desert Song*.

"Since the Bookshop I have almost conquered Anthony Lincoln. I have almost banished him. Well, almost. I attempt from love's sickness to fly and get quite a long way—but the trouble with Anthony is that he neither wants me nor wants to lose me; he won't let it be properly over until he chooses.

"I fear Cassie is having trouble with her Len."

"He got his motor bike, then," Elsie said.

She called round on a fine evening and she and Cassie were sitting with the door and window wide open. Miss Jean had gone to the theater with a new friend she had made through the bookshop—only a girl—Roddy was in bed, and in the sitting-room his mother was occupied in writing long letters to her sisters. Presently, no doubt, she would ask Cassie to take them to the post.

"Who did?" asked Cassie, as a matter of form.

"Len. Who else?"

"I didn't hear much about it."

"Alan got it him, secondhand. Very nice, he says."

"Fancy. And how's Alan?"

"He's fine. We went dancing up the Palais Saturday. That's the place! You and Len should ought to come with us sometime."

This was rather generous in Elsie, seeing the way Len danced, but it was not what concerned Cassie just then.

"When did he get the bike?"

"Len? Last Saturday, I think it was. Yes—must've been. They went out together Sunday to get him some practice."

"Did you get to see Ronald Colman this week?" Cassie asked.

"No. It was him or the Palais. But we're going to Greta Garbo, week after next."

Presently, as expected, Mrs. Garside looked into the kitchen with her letters. Elsie was leaving, anyway, and could have done the posting, but Cassie took the letters and they walked together to the pillar box. There Elsie stood talking about Alan while Cassie answered, Yes; No; I don't think so; and thought about Len.

At last they parted. "Keep your pecker up!" cried Elsie, as she swung across the road.

Halfway home, Cassie was overtaken by Mr. Anthony Lincoln, who came smiling to walk beside her.

"I'm just going your way. Is Mrs. Garside at home?"

"*Mrs.* Garside?"

"Mrs. Garside."

"Yes. She is. They're both in."

Miss Jean was watering the big pot of geraniums by the front door. She looked over her shoulder and saw who was coming, but turned back at once to pick off some dead leaves.

"Oh, hullo Anthony," she said, casually enough for Cassie's approval.

"Can I have a word with your mother, do you think?"

Miss Jean, though clearly as startled as Cassie had been, said, Yes, she was in the sitting room, go on in. . . . Cassie hoped she would continue with the watering can and the dead leaves, but after only a second's hesitation she put down the can and went indoors.

"Terribly sorry, old thing," he said. "I just want to speak to your mother quite privately."

With a rather flashing smile, instead of his usual confiding one, he went into the sitting room and closed the door behind him. Jean followed Cassie into the kitchen, saying in a rather high-pitched voice, "Well, how was your friend Elsie?"

"All right. She say Len have his motor bike. So that'll make him happy."

"You can go riding on the pillion."

"He never asked me yet. He never even told me."

The last postal delivery along Stanton Avenue came shortly after the final collection at the bottom of the road, and the postman's knock came as Jean and Cassie were talking, and while Anthony Lincoln was closeted with Mrs. Garside. Jean went to fetch the only letter and returned to the kitchen.

"They're *still* talking. Perhaps he's come to ask for my hand—what d'you think?" She gave a rather wild laugh and handed the letter. "It's for you."

Cassie had been taught that it was bad manners to open a letter in the middle of a conversation; so for that matter had Miss Jean Garside. So Cassie stood holding the letter politely and waiting for the right moment.

"I expect it's from home," Jean said. "I think letters are magic." And she went away.

Cassie still held the letter, looking at it from a distance. She did not know the writing. There was a London postmark. She knew it must be from Len and she wished she need not open it. The letter would tell her about the motor bike and she did not want to know. At last, with a feeling of doom and despair, she ran her thumb under the flap of the envelope and slowly tore it open.

Yes, it was from Len; yes, it was about the beautiful motor bike; about how much it had cost to buy, how much it would cost to run, about how it was best, Alan said, to get yourself insured against accidents—all very expensive. These details took the first sheet and half its back. In the second half of the second side, Len pointed out that he could not hope to afford a motor bike *and* a young lady, so he had had to choose. This took him to the bottom of the page, and the new sheet just said, "Perhaps things will get better soon until then Yours truly, Len."

It was just then that the sitting-room door opened and out came Anthony Lincoln, laughing and thanking Mrs. Garside for whatever it was he had sought from her. He was across the hall and out of the door, pulling it neat and sharp behind him, before Jean could reappear.

"Well, well," she said, moving into the kitchen once more. She looked at Cassie, and her tight-lipped expression broke up into a grin of sorts.

"Was your letter from home?"

Cassie shook her head. She stood there, just looking at Miss Jean, needing help, not knowing how to ask for it.

"What's the matter?"

Again Cassie just shook her head. Then she looked away and her shoulders began to shake, she dragged out a handkerchief from her apron pocket and cried into it with effortful silence, turning her back, abandoned and ashamed.

"Oh Cassie, don't! Is it Len?"

Cassie managed to nod.

"The letter! The letter was from Len?"

Silently Cassie groped on the table for the letter and without glancing at it, holding it as if it had been taken from some plague-stricken corpse, she handed it to Jean.

"Are you sure . . . ?"

Again the nod, while she blew her nose and tried to order herself a little.

"Oh!" cried Miss Jean, reading, fierce and furious. "Men!"

She put her hand awkwardly on Cassie's arm, and Cassie would gladly have turned and used the offered shoulder, only there was still just too much standing between them. However, she rallied a little under sympathy and went and washed her face at the sink.

"Have you got a plain postcard, Cassie?"

It seemed an odd thing to ask just then, but there was a packet of stamped cards that Gran had sent at Easter, stuck up behind the clock. Cassie reached for them dumbly.

Although the letter box on the corner had long been cleared, it was still possible to reply by return to a letter received by the last delivery. You simply walked to the post office and dropped it into the big box there, and it was sorted and sent on its way at midnight.

"You sit down now, Cassie, and write him an answer. I'll take it up to catch the late post. Just write: *Have a nice ride*, and sign it."

Cassie gave a gulping, half-hysterical laugh. She couldn't help thinking, even then, that Miss Jean was better at dealing with another girl's young man than with her own.

11

"WRITING THIS sort of journal is full of horrid pitfalls. Example, I am the heroine so I am almost bound to make myself nicer and everyone else much nastier than any of us really are. I have read quite a lot of diaries, and I can see that Pepys was his own hero, while John Evelyn was a hero only, as they say, *under God*: (Skipper of the barque so-and-so, under God. *See Hakluyt's Voyages.*) Fanny Burney is a heroine all right. . . . I say I have read quite a lot of diaries, but I believe it is really only those three—a dismal example of the point I have tried to make.

"Now I must write about Anthony. This is really why I set down the above. Because of my sudden awful insight. When it comes to Posterity—for which, or for whom, I am of course confidently writing—it or they will never be able to see how Anthony is so funny and very sweet in a lot of small ways, and sort of kind—though that is an odd thing to find myself writing at this precise moment. I expect it must be easier and more dramatic to write about quarrels and bad feeling; which no doubt is why the evil men do lives after them. When I write about D. I write about rows and things of that sort, whereas he is a person obviously very much loved by a lot of people—other actors tease him and grin at him; when he was in the army and only a ranker he seems to have looked after all the others. They called him Father. There is a wonderful poem written out in pencil on lined paper that he showed me once. It is addressed to him and called *Our Father*. He was about thirty at the time.

"This is me examining my conscience. The facts I write are all facts, but how can I know whether I am being fair? Every member of a family should keep a journal and then there should be a reading aloud on Sunday evenings (Idea for novel?). It is because of the Bartys that I begin to see more clearly—I *think*. Both of them, little old gray Barty and his tall smart sister, have set-to to change me in my own estimation. I am a new person in lots of ways. I am different. I swing along. I rush to work; I love every hour of it; almost, I come home reluctantly. I have written three more chapters of my novel that M. finds so horrid, and now I know I shall finish. I sing "Tom Bowling" all the time, in my mind if not out loud. It is the most melancholy tune I know and I only sing it when I am happy. This means I am happy in spite of Anthony, which is good.

"But I have to tell this thing about him, about how he came to the house this evening rather late and asked to see M. and was closeted with her while I tried to cheer up Cassie about Len—another story I must tell but not now. Anthony went away without a word to me, and after I had dashed to the post office with Cassie's reply to Len (a devastatingly simple message dictated by me; more later) M. was fidgeting about in the sitting room, and suddenly called me in.

166

" 'What did he want?' I asked, not meaning to mention him, even.

"I could see M. was dreadfully put out and she kept starting to say something and then it died away. It was most peculiar and mysterious.

" 'Well—what have you been talking about, all this time?'

"I know she likes him, though she worries that I like him too much. But he is ready to flirt, even with her—(not *even*—I don't really mean that) and of course she rather likes it, who wouldn't enjoy being made to feel young and attractive when they are over forty? But now she was angry. She was angry with Anthony. I think I must have known something rather nasty was coming, because I began to thump and thud inside my chest.

" 'He really is impossible, Jean.' She made it sound rather as if that was my fault. 'He came here saying he wanted my advice. He wanted my advice about a birthday present. Yes, I know what you're thinking and I don't wonder—that's what I thought. But it wasn't your birthday he was talking about. I'm sorry, darling, but you'd better know. He was talking about a girl called Yvonne something. It just happens that her birthday is a couple of days before yours.'

"I know this is rather a long bit of reported dialogue but I am not likely to forget anything she said. . . . It seems a pretty roundabout way of letting me know he's moved on and is busy elsewhere—though if anybody was to think of doing it that way I suppose it would be Anthony Lincoln.

"When she had told me this we were both very embarrassed. I daresay she expected me to cry, at the very least. It was marvelous that I didn't. I am still thinking about it.

" 'Oh well,' I said, 'they're all a bit mad in that household. Have you seen my library book?'

"After that I just went upstairs, humming—certainly not 'Tom Bowling,' though. 'Bye, bye Blackbird,' I think. More suitable.

"I am a much better actress now that I have stopped being one."

"We're both in the same boat," Miss Jean told Cassie at breakfast next morning. "Len's got a motor bike and Anthony Lincoln's got a girl called Yvonne. I think English people should have English names."

Cassie was at once touched by this confidence and shocked. Part of the shock was that Miss Jean could say out loud that she had, as you might say, been given the push. She flushed red as Jean spoke, in some strange way blushing for both of them.

Cassie had not meant to speak to Elsie of Jean's troubles. She successfully shrugged off Len, recalling with some irritation that she had been sorry for Elsie when she mislaid Alan—now Elsie was the perky one. Cassie tried to resist the temptation of being in the know about Jean and ignominiously, shamefully failed.

"That'll be Miss Yvonne Banks," Elsie decided. "The Richardsons are friendly with the Bankses. Well, I can tell you one thing, Cassie Martle—it won't last long."

"If that doesn't he'll be back," Cassie felt very gloomy.

"Mark my words," said Elsie, already triumphant. . . .

Soon they were moving from spring into early summer. Miles Garside's play ran on and on, surviving even two transfers, playing to big and appreciative houses. The summer, beginning with gray skies, now brightened and stirred. Cassie dreamed about her holiday and the Garsides visited the Lincolns as usual, the Lincolns visited the Garsides. Cassie had heard Mrs. Lincoln mocking Miss Jean for something or other and supposed she was out of favor with Anthony's mother as well as with Anthony who, twice so far, had brought Miss Yvonne Banks visiting. "How's the shop?" Mrs. Lincoln was asking once, when Cassie carried in coffee. It was amazing how she made it sound as if Miss Jean was selling cheap stockings.

Now it was mid-May, coming up to Whitsun, now it was June. The days were warm, but neither Cassie nor Miss Jean could absolutely enjoy them. More and more Cassie looked forward to going home, increasingly Jean was absorbed in her job, yet both were building over a pit and knew the structure might fold up and sink and disappear. One evening when the Garsides were out, he at the theater and she seeing the play for the twentieth or so time, Cassie answered the telephone and heard Anthony Lincoln asking for Miss Jean.

Jean was in her room; scribbling away, as Cassie would have said. She had to knock quite loudly before she was answered, and she wished she had not been answered at all. However, the message had be given once Jean had called, "Come in!"

"Mr. Lincoln on the phone, miss." She looked away at once, alarmed by the other girl's expression. "I'll tell him you're working."

"No! Wait. . . ." She must have seen in Cassie's face some reminder of the terse postcard sent to Len. . . . "Yes. All right. Jolly well tell him I'm working."

Cassie went downstairs sedately, picked up the telephone with measured movements, and with the utmost firmness, courtesy and conviction said, "Miss Jean's working, sir."

"Working? Oh. Oh I see. Did she say so?"

"Yes," said Cassie, dropping off the *sir*.

"I see. All right. I'll ring again later."

He hung up before she could tell him that Miss Jean usually worked until midnight. She did not see fit to carry the message that he would ring again and was relieved that Jean did not call down and ask her what he had said. She did, indeed, continue working, for at no other time when she was in her room was there such a total petrifying silence.

There was no further telephone call, but at half past ten or so, Anthony Lincoln appeared on the doorstep. Cassie was already halfway to bed, Jean answered the door, there was nothing to be done about it.

"Oh there you are," he said, coming inside without much encouragement on her part. "Look, Jean, I've got two tickets for the Albert Hall next Saturday afternoon. Can you come with me?"

"The Albert Hall? D'you mean *Hiawatha*?"

Standing at the top of the stairs Cassie could just see him taking out his wallet, waving the tickets at Jean.

"*Hiawatha.* Yes. What's wrong with that?"

"Well—isn't it a bit of a joke? I mean—aren't there a lot of amateurs?"

"It's a wonderful show," he said coldly.

"You've forgotten I work on Saturdays."

"Oh blast, you're always working. Well—daresay I can change them for the evening."

Cassie feared this might be too much for her, and it was.

"I'll look in my diary. It's in my handbag. I left it in the sitting room. I won't be a second."

It was noticeable that she did not ask him further than the hall, and he waited in a mannerly way until she called out—"Sorry. Something else to do."

"*What* else?"

He went into the sitting room, then, and Cassie could no longer hear what was being said, only a quick, angry-sounding exchange. Then Jean said, very loudly, "Oh, go to hell!" She came quickly out into the hall and Anthony followed.

"Jean?"

"Go to hell, I said!"

There was a moment's total silence. Then he flung across the hall, dragged the door open and pulled it crashing behind him. For good measure he slammed the front gate.

Jean was at the foot of the stairs and she called up, quite softly, "Are you there?"

"Yes, I am. I think the bang's woked up your brother."

"He'll soon go to sleep again. Did you hear?"

"Part—"

"Some people think they own the world, they really

171

do." She sat on the stairs and put her face down on her knees. "They think they own the whole blooming world and everybody in it. But they're wrong—they're really very wrong. . . . He left his wallet and the tickets. If he wants them he can fetch them, and if he fetches them— I'm out. You remember that."

"Yes, I'll remember." Cassie hesitated, then she said softly, "Are you all right, Miss Jean?"

"Yes, Cassie. *Yes*."

Next morning, there was an early breakfast for everyone. Mr. Garside's brother was selling his car and there was talk of Mr. Garside buying it. There was excitement. They had to go and see it, which meant a trip to the Bexhill area, but they could not be late back in London because Mr. Garside had of course an evening performance. These signs of renewed economic ease in the household pleased them all, including Cassie. She cooked everyone an extra rasher of bacon. Immediately after breakfast, Mr. and Mrs. Garside went off to catch a bus to the nearest tube station, which would take them to Victoria to catch a train to the Sussex coast.

"Next time we go to see David I'll drive you down, my dear," Mr. Garside promised.

They went off laughing, and Cassie thought they might be glad of a day to themselves—no keeping an eye on Roddy, no Miss Jean to quarrel with.

Jean watched her parents go, then prepared to rush up the road to catch her own bus in the opposite direction.

"Don't forget Roddy's going straight from school to the Richardsons' for tea, Cassie. Mind he doesn't forget Bruce's birthday present."

"I'll remember. . . . You'll be late if you don't watch out."

For some reason, the fine morning, perhaps, Cassie followed Jean out to the gate and closed it after her. Then she stood watching her legging it up the road, tall and purposeful, as if nothing could cancel the fact that she was setting out to have a marvelous day. And just as if she knew Cassie would be standing there, Jean turned at the corner and waved before she dashed across the road to catch the bus. . . .

Just as Cassie was going back into the house, shooing in the cat, which had followed her and was pretending it loved her, Anthony Lincoln came tearing round the corner and up the road to No. 15. He braked with a flourish and a scream of tires, and shouted out to Cassie—

"Did Miss Jean find my wallet?"

"Yes, she did. I'll get it."

She ran back into the house and into the sitting room. There lay the wallet, smooth black leather, A.L. stamped in gold on the corner.

Rather to her annoyance, he followed her in. When she turned with the wallet in her hand he had come in and was standing by the door.

"I suppose she's gone? Miss Jean, I mean."

"Yes, she has. . . . This is it, isn't it?"

"Oh yes—it is. Thanks, Edith. Thank you. Is it today Mr. and Mrs. Garside are going to Bexhill? I could give them a lift to Victoria."

"They've left," she said; and immediately knew she had made a bad mistake.

At this moment Roddy came thumping down the

173

stairs, shouted out good-bye to Cassie and rushed away, banging the front door so that the house shook and shivered much as it had done on Anthony's exit the previous evening.

"There goes the Garside handful!" cried Anthony.

"He's a very nice little boy, sir."

Anthony was shuffling the two tickets between his fingers. "You have them," he said, holding them out to Cassie.

She could not help the little jump of excitement. If only she and Elsie could go together. . . .

"I'm not off Saturdays, though."

"Ask Mrs. Garside."

"My friend'd have to ask her lady, too. I don't expect it can be managed, thank you very much, Mr. Lincoln."

"Tell you what," he said. "Ask Mrs. Garside for the afternoon off—and come with me!"

He made it sound a bit of a joke, a sort of spree, as Elsie would say, but Cassie was shocked.

"No, thank you."

"Why not? I've seen you on your day out, Edith. You look very smart. I'd like to take you."

"No. Thank you all the same."

"Change your mind. Go on."

"I've said no. Take your wallet and go. You'll be late at your office."

She knew she had made another mistake. The words, too familiar altogether, had removed the conventional barrier between them.

He held out his hand for the wallet.

"You're a very pretty girl, Edith—anyone tell you? I must say I like pretty girls best."

"Fancy that, sir."

It was too late, however, to get back to such forms. As Anthony took the wallet he took her hand as well. The wallet dropped back on to the table it had occupied all night. He held her at arm's length in a teasing way, and she could just see what it was Miss Jean found attractive about him—and lots of other girls, by the way he was behaving. She knew she could still get away quite easily if she kept her head. In spite of this certainty, she began to struggle and pick at his hand round her wrist.

"Please don't!" she cried. "What would Miss Jean think?"

"Who? Who's Miss Jean?"

She made her free hand into a fist and thumped him on the chest. It was her left hand and struck with the muffled force of a hand in some quicksands dream. They began tussling in a stupid way that gradually slipped from laughter on his side into annoyance. On hers there was a fully grown angry hatred, and because of it she let the situation right out of her control. Now he would never let her go easily.

She thought she heard the gate slam and jerked up her head to listen. At once there was a great banging on the front-door knocker and the bell furiously rung.

"Roddy! That's Roddy!"

Almost immediately, the boy came and banged on the window, shouting out, "Cassie! Cassie! I forgot Bruce's present! Buck up—I'll be late! Cassie. . . ."

"Oh damn it," Anthony said, quite mildly. He let her go and was ahead of her to the door. "Hullo there, Roddy old man."

"Hullo. . . . What are you . . . ?"

"Where did you leave the parcel, dear?" Cassie asked, drawing the breath up with difficulty from under her ribs. "Is it in your room?"

"Yes, I. . . . What was he doing? What were you doing in there?"

"Mr. Lincoln left something behind, just like you. Quick now. You'll be in trouble at school."

She chivvied him up the stairs, found the parcel, urged him down again. The front door stood open. The car was gone.

"He might've given me a lift."

"Never mind. You run, now."

"He goes right past. . . . He's a beast."

"Yes," she said. "He is."

"Cassie—?"

"Now what?"

"Nothing." He had that way of flinging his arms round her, hugging without kissing, and he did so now.

"There," she said, holding him close for a second. "That's nice. Off you go! Don't dawdle, now!"

When the door had slammed behind him she began to shiver. She went into the kitchen and leaned against the table, hearing him say "Who? Who's Miss Jean?" and feeling that hot flood of hatred.

After a bit, she got herself a glass of water and by the time she had washed and dried the glass and replaced it

176

automatically in its cupboard, she knew what she was going to do.

"I shall now go," she said out loud.

At once she went upstairs to her room and pulled out the basket in which she had brought her clothes here over a year ago. Where were those clothes now? She had discarded them all save the one petticoat, kept because Marge had made it and taken such care to sew lace round the neck and armholes, and even round the hem. Cassie began to change, tossing away the silk undies, as Elsie called them, pulling on the petticoat. But after that she was obliged to get into her smart London clothes that she had bought with such delight, saving for them, choosing them, lingering over the choice.

She got out her purse and emptied it on to the bed, then the contents of the little cash box. There was only one pound note, the rest small stuff—four sixpences, three shillings, three half-crowns. Not enough. Not nearly enough for her fare—first the bus, then the underground, then the train; then, with luck, the afternoon bus at the other end. No one would be there to meet her, for no one would know that they should.

Cassie went into Miss Jean's room. On the dressing table there was an old chocolate box, with the head of King George on an embossed coin, a great big sovereign, and red ribbon with a bow. Cassie knew that there was money in the box, because she had seen Jean before now put in odd coins or take them out, and she had often left the lid off. Cassie herself had found this very careless, but now she was glad she knew what was inside. She took the lid from the box. There were three pound notes there, each folded rather childishly into four. Cassie took the notes and put them in her handbag that she and Elsie had chosen together in Swan & Edgar's. Then she found a piece of paper in Jean's desk, which was open as usual, with the flap down. She sat down to write with Jean's own pen that wrote all her stories and her huge great journal.

"Forgive me, I had to," wrote Cassie, "I will send a P.O. for the £3." She paused and then she wrote again, "Forgive me please it was nothing I do." She changed *do* to *did*, and then concluded, "Your loving Cassie."

She sat there at the desk, looking round the room, looking and looking, knowing she would never come to this house again, never again laugh with Jean Garside in the pleasant kitchen at 15, Stanton Avenue, London S.W. . . . Then she thought if the wallet was still lying on the table in the sitting-room—surely Miss Jean need never know that Anthony Lincoln had come to fetch it and then found other things to do. . . . But this comfort could not last her long. Roddy had seen Anthony and spoken to him, and it was not possible to know what he had seen when he came banging on the window.

Now Cassie left Jean's room and went downstairs, and this time she wrote in the kitchen, sitting at the table as so often, on her own paper that was pink, with lined envelopes.

"Madam, I have now gone home, there is no trouble there but I have to go. Thank you, Edith." Again she wished she could say more, but she did not know how.

She read the note twice and thought little of it. As last she put a PS. "Thank you very much indeed." And underlined it. She left the note in its nice envelope propped up on the kitchen table.

After that there was nothing more to stay for. She left with the clothes she stood up in, and in her handbag the one thing she felt able to take away. It was the book Jean had given her for Christmas. She had not read any of it, but one day she might like to. Anyway, Miss Jean had written in it, *To Cassie*, and then had signed her own name; so it seemed to belong to both of them.

It was hot in the train and even before they had pulled out of the main station Cassie felt that she had traveled a long way. She had had no second thoughts, not even of going only as far as Dad's; Mum would have sent her back, would have gone with her, maybe. As they dragged out of sprawling London, Cassie sat wondering if she had chosen the right words for her two hasty messages, words that they would understand. When she sent back the money to Miss Jean, and she knew the family would help her with this, just as they had all helped Jack, she would try to write a proper letter and explain a bit—though she must try not to hurt Miss Jean by saying too much about Mr. Lincoln; it would have been good to be able to warn her, but perhaps she was warned by now—perhaps if Roddy told his tale, she would understand. Mrs. Garside, perhaps, would never understand. She would speak of ingratitude. She might cry to Jean, as Cassie had heard her about someone else, "What ideas have you been putting in her head?" Her daughter would reply as she had replied on another occasion: "That's what heads are for." It comforted her to remember that she had stood at the gate that morning to wave to Jean, and Jean had waved back. It was as if they had both known.

The last part of the journey was slow. It was mid-afternoon, very hot, and Cassie had not eaten since breakfast. The train shuffled into small stations and paused. No one got on and no one got off. Only a silent flag wafted them on their way, the empty platform sliding away, carrying with it a smell of tar melted by the heat.

At last the train speeded up slightly, becoming again altogether more important, and when it arrived at the much larger getting-out station there was at once some bustle and shouting to brisk up the proceedings. As Cassie had hoped, the afternoon bus was still standing in the station yard, with the usual two or three taxis and a couple of pony-traps. The bus waited patiently for the privilege of trundling on their way Cassie Martle, one schoolboy with a bulging satchel, an old woman with an empty basket, a man reading the afternoon racing news in an early evening paper. She did not know them, they did not know her. A great isolation swept over her, not loneliness, not regret, but a feeling of existing all alone in the world, in which she moved on feet that barely touched the ground.

She alone got off at the crossroads, and paused a moment, wondering which of two ways to choose—the quickest, or the prettiest. She chose the prettiest. First it would bring her to the river and then by Mr. Clare's fine acres to the footbridge, and so by a field footpath to her own home.

Now, as she walked slowly under the sun, the feeling of having a tight chain wound round her heart began to ease, and very gradually she began to escape the bondage that had been laid on her by that morning's doings. As she walked her shoes grew smaller, and presently she took them off and carried them, walking in her stockings for a time. But when she came to the river bank she sat down and peeled off her stockings, too. Leaning out over the water she dropped them gently and saw them swirled around then carried lazily to entangle with a floating swag of weed. She was wearing a little tip-tilted hat with flowers under the brim, and she took it off, and sat there holding it for a moment, for she had coveted and then achieved it. Then she spun it away from her like a plate, and it, too, whirled giddily for a moment, then more sedately, bobbing a little, sailed away. Cassie knew, as she threw away her stockings and her hat, that she had begun to throw away Edith, that stranger who had lived beside her for a year and more. So she tossed her shoes one by one after the rest. They filled and sank.

Gradually Cassie began to peel off the clothes she had loved so well—the tightish dress with the low neck, too warm for the day, the white gloves, the brassiere and the girdle that Elsie had said every decent girl needed—until she sat in the petticoat she had brought from home and felt the late afternoon sun on her skin, the harsh dry earth beneath her feet, under her hands.

The fine weather of the last few weeks had brought on

the poppies. Here at the river's verge the cornfields hung back a little and the poppies flowed into the spaces that were left, hanging out above the water, bunching and falling in prodigal masses right down to the very margin, to mingle there with purple vetch and with daisy, heartsease and the scented plants of camomile that would not flower till after every poppy but a few stragglers had come and gone.

Cassie lay back at the side of the path, among green corn and red poppies, and the sun fidgeted into her hair. A grasshopper leaped from her forehead to the outstretched palm of her hand and so on its way, strong and purposeful. For a time she lay staring upward, watching those vapors that were barely seen yet carried many birds upon their back—two kestrel and a sparrow hawk, and a flight of lapwing caught up in passing, and questing, screaming swallows darting at flies. Among the field growth there was a steady murmur and rhythm that got into her head. With the scent of poppies it made her drowsy. She closed her eyes, and forgetting everything between then and now, she slept.

A voice called her awake and she knew well before she opened her eyes whose voice it must be. This was Mr. Clare's ground, after all, and though her feet had led her, they had taken the path she chose.

"Cassie," said Ned. "Cassie Martle. Time you woke up, bor."

Cassie opened her eyes but did not move. She knew about her petticoat and her bare feet but there seemed little to care about in that. Soon she would move, but not yet. But she turned her head very slightly and smiled at Ned. At first his expression did not change, but then he smiled, too.

"Mr. Clare think happen some lady was set on to drown herself—all of them fine clothes floating."

She spoke, then, asking, was he surprised?

"What's surprising? That you come home?"

"It might be."

"Come by bus from the station, didn't you? Sam Suttle see you there. Anyone know you come home?"

Casise sat up, not knowing whether to feel cheated of one thing, or rewarded by another.

"Gran'll be cross with me, will she?"

"First off, maybe." He laughed. He was squatting down beside her and she saw his face and everything in it laid so bare she was obliged to look away—though smiling as she did so.

She rose, winced at a stone, then laughed for the pleasure of it.

"I dare you take me home in my petticoat, Ned Gooderham."

He grinned, then. "Come on, you. I'll dare you dare me!"

He put his arm round her and dipped his cheek briefly against her hair and said no more.

They went slow and slower along the river path, and so over the footbridge, forgetting Mr. Clare, who must by now be thinking his laborer had drowned himself along with the nameless woman. Then there was the cut across the far field, then the gap in Gran's back hedge. They went in past the dead bonfire and the peasticks from last year, the pile of broken clay pots, the cabbage stalks rotting on the heap. The hens ran out to gossip round their ankles and Gran, hearing the noise, called out as usual from inside the cottage—

"Who's there?"

"Gran," Cassie called back, "it's me."

BARBARA WILLARD's first novels were for adults, but in 1958 she wrote a book she describes as "about children. I realized the best sort of children's books would be about children doing things any child could do—not finding buried treasure or spy-catching or any of those worn-out things." Today Barbara Willard is one of England's foremost writers of children's books and the recipient of the Guardian Award for her Mantlemass novels, which have also been pubished with success in the United States.

Like Miles Garside in *The Country Maid*, Barbara Willard's father was an actor. And like Jean Garside, Barbara Willard acted during her teenage years. Unlike Jean, however, Barbara Willard played more substantial roles—that of Macduff in *Macbeth*, for instance.

After she left school, Barbara Willard found it difficult to choose between writing and acting as a career, and so she did both until writing won out.